Windsong Summer

by PATRICIA CECIL HASS

Cover illustration by Tran Mawicke

SCHOLASTIC BOOK SERVICES
NEW YORK • TORONTO • LONDON • AUCKLAND • SYDNEY • TOKYO

To my father

ISBN 0-590-30879-3

12 11 10 9 8 7 6 5 4 3 2 1   4   0 1 2 3 4 5/8

Printed in the U. S. A.   06

Metric Conversions

The measurements in this book are given in inches, feet, yards, and miles. For readers who use the metric system of measurement, here are some helpful conversions:

1 inch = about 2.54 centimetres

1 centimetre = about .4 inch

1 foot = about 30.5 centimetres or .3 metre

1 metre = about 3.3 feet or 1 yard

1 yard = about 91.44 centimetres or .91 metre

1 mile = about 1609.3 metres or 1.6 kilometres

1 kilometre = about .62 mile

One

Tim rolled over on his stomach and peered through the white slats of the swimming raft. At first the water only looked dark green, but in a minute, when he tried squinting, he could see bottom, fifteen feet below. Yellow bars of sunlight hit the surface on either side of the raft, lighting up the water all the way down.

"Cool," Tim said, looking at a big orange and black striped fish.

"What?" said his sister, Mouse, who was trying to get on the raft by doing kick jumps out of the water.

"Some kind of fish." Tim pushed his dark hair out of his eyes. "It probably has teeth, the kind you see strung up on people's walls, or made into necklaces."

Mouse stopped jumping and hung onto the raft, drops of water glistening on her arms. "Those are sharks' teeth, I think. How big is it?"

"Medium. It's gone," Tim said. He stood up

and tried to see if he could get his big toe through an especially large crack between the boards.

"You'll get stuck." Mouse was watching from below. "Dad'll have to come out and saw off your foot."

"Good," Tim said. "Maybe to make up for having no foot he'd let us do something about a boat."

Mouse let go and began treading water. "He won't," she said. "Not until the new office is started, anyway."

Their parents' plan to spend the summer in the Caribbean had seemed wonderful when they were at home in Chicago. Their father, a mining engineer, had been assigned to open a research office in the West Indies for his large minerals firm, and their mother, a mineralogist, was helping with the project. Chicago was 800 miles inland, and although Tim and Mouse had been to its lake beaches, they had never seen the ocean before, except in the movies.

But now that they were here, they felt frustrated because their parents were so busy. Tim looked at the mountains that stretched around the huge bay, and the horizon far beyond the reefs. Clear blue-green water beckoned in every direction, backed by soft white beaches ringed with palm trees.

"A whole tropical island, a big one," Tim said. "There must be a million things we could do here with a boat. Even a rowboat."

Mouse looked at him. Her hair, dark streaky blonde, floated in the water around her shoulders. "We're doing things now," she said. "We're swimming. And don't forget what Captain Fisher said."

Captain Fisher was an old friend of their father's. The two men had gone to school together. For many years Captain Fisher had lived on the island, running a large boatyard, with a diving and salvage business on the side. He had helped the Randolphs find a place to stay and had offered, when they were settled, to take them fishing in one of his boats.

"That could be a while," Tim said. "It's now I'm thinking about."

He stood up and began to edge along the raft, curling his toes over the side to keep his balance. "Whoever falls off first loses," he said, going faster.

Mouse scrambled up the ladder. She was eleven but small for her age, and sometimes she had trouble following Tim, who was a year older and considerably taller.

At first she only managed to walk fast, using her arms to balance, but soon they were both tearing around the slippery surface, until to Mouse it seemed a whirling white blur, and Tim saw only the mountains and the sunlit water in a cartwheel of blue and purple. He fell in, shouting.

"You jumped on purpose," Mouse said, flopping her arms to stand straight. "I was ahead. So I won."

"I was hot. Anyway, it's a dumb game." Tim was watching some fishing sloops, far out by the reef. He wondered what it would be like to be that far out, and how the bay would look from there.

Mouse lowered herself slowly on the rocking raft and sat with her legs in the clear water. She could see a pink shell on the white sandy bottom, and she watched it move slowly along.

"It's getting late." Tim's voice sounded far away. "We'd better go."

"Okay." Mouse stood up. Suddenly she felt full of energy. "Yiii!" she shouted, and she flung herself out off the raft as far as she could. Down, down she went into the cooler water below the surface, then up again to break into the dazzling warmth of the glittering afternoon. Tim was already swimming, heading for shore, but he turned on his back and kicked water at her.

"Race you in," he shouted.

Mouse put her head down and took off, churning through the water after him. "Go, go, go," she said in her mind as she kicked, keeping her strokes even, breathing in rhythm. But it didn't work. He was much faster and, besides, he was far ahead.

"I won!" she could hear him shouting, as he reached shallow water and splashed out onto the sand.

"Who cares," Mouse thought, but she kept her head low and swam doggedly on. She was getting tired of the way he was always using her to test himself, but there was nothing she could do until she grew more.

She reached the pale line where the water joined the sand, and ran to pick up her towel. Tim was already jogging along the wide beach below their hotel. The hotel was small, built in open levels on the side of a hill in a way that took advantage of the island's natural greenery, and the prevailing breezes from the bay. There were steps cut in the rocks which led up to the main terrace, and Tim waited for Mouse at the bottom.

"I'm starving." Mouse started up the steps.

"Mmn," Tim said. He had been thinking about food too, but it was because he was wondering if he would gain any weight down here. His nickname at school was Bean, short for bean pole, and he hated what it stood for — tall and skinny. Weak, he thought.

"I'm going to start eating only meat," he said.

"Why?" Mouse sounded out of breath.

"For the protein. To build my muscles." He stopped climbing and draped his towel around and flexed his arms. "Just in case anything happens."

Mouse laughed. "You'd better eat a lot, then. In a place like this, I have a feeling something really exciting is going to."

Rolf rolled over slowly and opened his eyes. He could hear the water slapping gently on the sand beside him. Above, the sky was turning pink from the sunset. He sat up.

"Time to go, Zec," he said to a sea gull walking nearby on the beach. "Wind's going."

The pink light turned the palm trees behind the sand to gold, and Rolf stretched his arms forward and looked at the light on his tan. It made him look rose coloured.

Then he looked out to sea, and yawned. "The bay looks empty, Zec. We can sail there now and have it all to ourselves."

The sea gull made mewing noises, like a cat crying, and Rolf got up. His bare feet made little hollows in the sand at the water's edge, and gurgled in the water as he walked out to his boat.

He swung aboard and began setting sail. The sea gull flew from the beach to the cabin, and then to Rolf's shoulder, and the boy left the sails and walked back to the cockpit.

Now the sails luffed and the boat backed quietly, sliding over the still lavender water. In a minute she caught a puff of air and turned, heading along the cove for the open bay. On the beach the palm trees swung gently, while the water oozed over Rolf's footprints until they disappeared.

He let the boat go almost free, following the current, and lay back in the cockpit, watching the sky. But suddenly he saw that the sea gull on the mast was cocking its head, and the boy looked forward.

A half mile away along the reef, several men were working, loading nets and baskets into two motor launches. Rolf knew who they were, coral and sponge divers who worked for the big seaman, Captain Fisher.

"Darn, Zec," he said. "They might see us. We'll have to wait."

He held his boat close inside the cove, shading his eyes while he watched the men packing up for the day. In a few minutes they had loaded everything into the boats, and Rolf could hear the motors start. He watched the launches move away from the reef and purr rapidly across the bay toward the main island. Then he stood up, idly turning his face back and forth against the breeze, feeling its coolness.

He waited until the boats had disappeared out of sight into the jaws of the town docks far away, and then put his foot on the tiller and gave it a push.

"Now we can sail, Zec," he said. "There'll be a breeze in the bay for an hour more, anyway."

"Hey!" Tim looked up from his dessert. He had changed his mind about eating only meat when he saw the strawberry shortcake, with mounds of whipped cream spread all over the plate.

"Look at that boat!" Mouse had seen it too, a small sailboat with a bright white sail, crossing the bay.

"It looks empty," their mother said.

"It's not. There's somebody in the back, I think," Tim said while Dad signed the check. "What kind of boat is it, Dad?"

Mr. Randolph turned and looked out at the bay. "It's a sloop. Nice looking, too. Come on. Had enough to eat?"

Tim finished his last bite and he and Mouse got up and went to the edge of the terrace. The bay curved in under the seawall, and there was a rail that prevented people from falling off into the water. They hung over the edge, watching the boat, and Mouse climbed on the rail to see better. Mrs. Randolph strolled over and gave her a hug.

"Be careful. If you fall in, Dad would have to jump in and fish you out, and he's all dressed up. We've got to go to a party."

"Oh, no!" Tim said. "You mean we'll just have to sit here?"

"I know, I hate to leave you," Mrs. Randolph said. "But the people we need to see are scattered around the island, and the easiest way for us to meet them is in the evening, at parties. Anyway, tomorrow night we're taking you to Captain Fisher's."

Tim brightened. "I hope he says something about going on a boat."

"He probably will," Mom said.

Mouse got down and the three of them stood watching the last of the sun above the mountains on the other side of the bay, and the sailboat, nearly opposite them now. It looked different from the island fishing sloops, its lines slimmer and cleaner. The dark blue hull seemed to gleam in the dying light.

"Why, I think it's someone your age," Mom said. "It looks like a boy."

"Or a pygmy," Mouse said. "Maybe he's an advance scout, planning an attack. Then when it's dark the whole tribe'll come, and while you and Dad are gone they'll swarm ashore and kidnap everybody in the hotel, one by one."

"'And a wolf stole back, and a wolf stole back, to carry the word to the waiting pack,'" Mom quoted. "That's from *The Jungle Book*. Didn't you have it in school?"

"I've forgotten everything I learned in school," Tim said. "I'm thinking about here."

"I've read it. I liked it," Mouse said. She clutched the railing. "Maybe they won't kidnap us, maybe they'll adopt us. And we can go live with them in the mountains, eating grass."

Mom laughed. "I hope not. I'd miss you, and anyway Tim says he needs meat."

"Yes," Mouse said. "Human heads."

"Mouse!" Mom made a face.

Tim was still watching the boat. "He does look like he's our age. I can see him. He's got light hair."

"Are you people coming?" Dad called. "We'll be late, Margaret."

They left the terrace and went into the hotel lobby, which was really more like a porch. It, too, was strung along the railing, only separated from the dining room by a bamboo wall.

"Now," Dad said, "no more pillow fights, and no more loud singing. Those people in the next room complained, I think. The manager mentioned it to me this morning. If we're going to be here all summer we don't want to antagonize people in the hotel."

"We can live on the beach," Mouse said.

"Amanda." Mouse's real name was Amanda, but no one ever called her that but Mom. When she did, the children knew she was getting really mad.

"Right, Dad, we won't," Tim said. "It's just that we want to do stuff with you."

"I know," Dad said. "And I do too. But for the time being we'll have to make do with our boring, day to day lives." He grinned. "And

I'd say they're not too bad at the moment, are they?"

Tim and Mouse shook their heads.

"It's too bad there aren't any children your age staying here," Mom said. "But since there aren't, play some games. There must be some in the game room."

"Parcheesi and dominoes," Mouse said.

"Wow. Big deal," Tim muttered. Luckily Mom didn't hear. She nodded and kissed them.

"Have fun," she said. "See you in the morning."

There was a television set in the hotel, in the lobby, but it only got one fuzzy channel from Trinidad. Tonight it wasn't working at all. There wasn't anything to read either, but Tim and Mouse found a pack of cards in a table drawer. For an hour they played fish and rummy, and then they went upstairs to bed.

While Mouse was brushing her teeth in the little sink in their room, Tim stood on a chair, trying to reach the ceiling with a stick and dislodge a small green chameleon. The lizard saw him and every time the stick came near, it calmly moved away.

"He's waiting for dark, to kill us," Tim said in a spooky voice, and Mouse shuddered.

The light was almost gone outside. She wondered if the lizard might really drop down on her bed in the dark. Then she remembered the mosquito nets that covered their beds.

"He can't get at us," she said.

Tim went and stood on the balcony, open to the sea. Below he could hear the clink of dishes and the voices of a few late eaters.

"I wonder who that boy was."

"A pygmy." Mouse saw Tim's disgusted expression and added, "I mean, I don't think he was a tourist."

"No. Well, he's lucky." Tim came back into the room and threw himself backward on the mattress, and began to bounce up and down. He found he could get higher if he used his elbows to propel with.

"You're making a thumping noise," Mouse said. "Those people will complain again."

"They'd better not," Tim said, but he lay still anyway. After a minute he said, "You know what?"

"What?"

"I don't want just to go out with Captain Fisher on his boats. What we need is a boat of our own. Like that boy had."

"I know," Mouse agreed. "Except we don't know how to sail."

"We could learn," Tim said. He got up and turned out the light, and got back on his bed, sitting up. Dappled moonlight poured through the balcony, and fell across his determined face. "All we have to do is persuade Dad."

"Umn." Mouse sounded thoughtful in the shadows. "How?"

"I don't know, but I'm going to talk to him." Tim lay down with a thump. "First thing in the morning."

Two

But at breakfast, Dad was in a bad mood.

"If these landowners would only cooperate," he was saying to his wife as Tim and Mouse sat down at the table. "How can we find the metal if they won't even let us on their land? What's more, they don't even seem interested."

"Perhaps we should cable the home office," Mrs. Randolph said.

"That's not the point, Meg." Mr. Randolph attacked his melon with his spoon. "We've got to get it arranged from this end. That's why we're here."

"Yes, darling, I know," Mom said. "It *is* difficult. Eat your egg, Mouse." Mouse hated eggs, but now she ate hers. She could tell from the conversation that something had gone wrong at the party last night, and this was not the morning to make anyone mad.

Tim waited until the waiter had poured his parents' coffee, steaming hot and black. Then he took a deep breath.

"Dad, do you remember that boat last night?"

His father looked up, distracted. "The sailboat we saw at dinner?"

"Yes, with the boy in it. Well," Tim hurried on, "since he was by himself, it can't be too dangerous to go out alone. You're really busy, and I think we could handle a boat ourselves, without waiting for you."

Dad frowned.

"Tim." He leaned forward. "No. First of all, you don't know how to sail, and it's a real skill. Second, any kind of boat is dangerous down here, even a rowboat, unless you know what you're doing. There're bad reefs and shoals close in, and if you capsize out in the bay it's very deep, very deep."

"Well, can we find out about boat lessons, then?" Tim said. "There must be some place a guy'll teach us how. We don't know when you'll have time."

"That's right," his father said. "But anything like lessons would be too expensive. When I have time I'll teach you myself, and meanwhile please don't bring it up again."

"That's that," Mouse muttered under her breath.

"The hotel rents bikes," Mr. Randolph was

saying. "Or you can play tennis." There was a sandy tennis court beyond the hotel garden.

"We can play tennis at home." Tim felt his stubborn streak rising. "It's more fun around the water."

"Or take a picnic up the beach," Mrs. Randolph suggested. "We can get you a lunch from the hotel kitchen." She pushed back her chair and looked up at the sunshine. "It's a beautiful morning. If Dad and I didn't have a meeting in town, I think we'd take the day off ourselves."

"Speaking of which, Meg" — Mr. Randolph looked at his watch — "we'd better leave. It's nine-thirty."

Mrs. Randolph got up and smoothed Tim's hair as though to straighten out his tense face. Mouse jumped up too, upsetting her milk. She tried to mop it up but only sloshed it more.

"Never mind," Mom said, helping her. "Go get your bathing suits while I ask for your lunch."

Ten minutes later she met them in the lobby with a wicker basket of sandwiches, and handed them a tube of sunburn cream.

"Put it on thick, please," she said. "July sun in the tropics is no joke." She gave them one of her sudden, warm smiles. "And stop pushing so about the boats, will you? Dad and I are under a lot of pressure. This is a big job down here, and it means a lot to both of us to do it well."

Mouse nodded. "Okay."

Tim was thinking that sometimes his mother had a way of making him feel he was about eight years old, shouting for a cookie. It was a feeling he didn't like because he knew she was right. "Okay," he said. "We'll be fine."

"Good." Mom kissed them. "Have a good day. Don't forget we're taking you to Captain Fisher's tonight at six."

She left, waving, and Mouse and Tim watched the car out of sight. Then they picked up their things and went down the cliff steps. Tim jumped the last six feet, and when Mouse reached him at the bottom, he was looking thoughtfully around.

"Don't just stand there," she said impatiently. "Come on!"

"I'm thinking of where to go," he said. "We don't want to stay here and be tourists, like those people." He gestured at the hotel beach, with its gaudy, striped umbrellas and a few oiled guests lying on the sand.

Mouse turned around, looking up the coast. "We can still explore, even without a boat," she said. "First the beaches, and then we can move inland, like Robinson Crusoe. Let's start beyond those rocks we saw from the raft."

"Hey." Tim looked at her. "You've been thinking. Very good."

She made a face at him and handed him the basket. "Very good." Her tone mimicked his. "All my ideas are good. Most of them are better than yours."

"Hah," he said, but he sounded cheerful.

They jogged to the end of the hotel beach, away from the town. The big rocks stretched across the sand, piled helter-skelter over each other in a long line out to sea. The coral surfaces were slippery from salt water, and even wearing tennis shoes, climbing up on them was scary. Spray flew up in Tim's face, and Mouse looked uneasily at the waves crashing with a booming sound below. They scrambled and jumped from boulder to boulder, teetering on one last giant with a knife-edged top. Beyond that it was lower, and finally an easy jump to the sand on the other side.

This beach was deserted. The water was still and inviting, and the pink sand was untouched, almost waiting for their footprints. Mouse felt a wild surge of joy, looking at it. "I love it here," she said.

Tim was looking at a house on the hill behind, nearly hidden in tall tropical trees. "Who do you think lives up there?"

"The local chief. He's probably watching us."

"Act normal, then," Tim said. "Don't let him know what we're doing."

Mouse laughed. "We aren't doing anything yet."

"We still shouldn't be noticed," Tim said, "just in case."

"Walk in the water, then," she said, "so we won't leave tracks."

They waded, following smooth underwater ridges of sand that felt soft under their feet. Little fish darted away from their legs, bright-coloured and transparent. Tim stepped in a hole and wet his shorts, but the water was so warm it was like a bath, and they went out up to their waists, taking turns balancing the picnic basket on their heads. Mouse saw a whole school of bigger fish following them. "Look."

Tim turned around and walked backward, kicking water high in the air. It sparkled in the sun, and the fish, still following, jumped up for it like food.

Suddenly Mouse realized that the clear

water was an endless world for fish, a whole new place she had never thought about. Her eyes swept farther, all the way to the horizon. "They can go anywhere, without having to stop," she said.

She leaned down and put her face in and opened her eyes. Surprisingly, the water seemed less clear from underneath. She came up, sputtering.

At the far end of the beach they splashed to the sand, and into a grove of palm trees. Behind the trees was a cliff, carved by the waves from ancient coral rock. Mouse liked the way it looked, weathered in the sun to a pale hard silver. "How high do you suppose it is?" she said.

"Let's find out. We can leave the basket here and come back for it."

Tim put their lunch in the shade beside a tiny pool in some rocks. They started up the cliff, searching for handholds, digging in with their toes. It was a harder climb than it looked, but finally they stood beside each other on a ledge just under the top, feeling the cool wind blow across their shoulders. They looked up, watching the puffy white clouds racing across the sky. Below they could see the beach they had just come over, and beyond that the rocks and the hotel. The umbrellas looked like striped mushrooms from here, and the people like black dots in the white sand. Far in the distance was the western arm of the bay with its mountains, and in front was the reef, far out.

"That bay's ten miles across, I bet," Tim said.

The rest of the cliff slanted up behind them just enough to block the view in the other direction. "I think we can get up there," Tim said. "We can probably see for miles."

He scrabbled at the ledge and heaved himself up, kicking and straining. Mouse shook her hair out of her face, looking up. She loved to squint through her eyelashes and feel the hot sun on her eyelids.

"Are you coming?" Tim's voice was blown away by the wind.

She opened her eyes, and saw several sea gulls wheeling farther out on the cliff. They were screaming harshly, and swooping over something, but she couldn't see what it was because it was lower down in a hollow of the rocks.

"Tim! Wait! There's something out there."

He turned and looked in the direction she pointed.

"They're after another gull," he called. He eased himself back down and went out to the ledge toward the birds. In a minute he saw the trouble. "I think it's hurt. It can't fly."

The gull on the rocks was hissing at its fellows in the air, wings half raised and drawn back, darting its beak forward in vicious thrusts when one came too close.

"We'd better rescue it," Tim called. "Maybe it needs a vet."

He had almost reached the place now, and the bird saw him, turning its baleful beak in his direction. It began to mew and squawk, walking away from the hollow, farther out on the cliff. Tim came back to Mouse.

"It's got one of their fish," he said. "I think that's why they're after it. Listen, if you come out and get on one side and keep its attention, I can throw my shirt over it and catch it."

Mouse nodded. She crept behind Tim along the ledge, not daring to look down. Once she couldn't help it, and she had a glimpse of feathery green, the tops of the palm trees below, that made her stomach turn over. She turned her eyes away and started forward again.

Tim wormed away at an angle, keeping low. When he reached a big rock he stopped, crouched behind it. Mouse tried a squawk to get the bird to notice her. She sounded queer, but it worked. The gull turned and looked at her. She saw Tim worming forward, his blue shirt in his hands, and then suddenly she heard a shout.

A boy, barefoot and darkly tanned, with blond hair bleached straw-white by the sun, was poised on the far side of the cliff. He stood there an instant, and then he hurled himself on Tim.

They rolled over and over. Mouse shrieked at them, but the wind tore the words from her mouth. Now the boy was on top of Tim, pulling on the shirt, hitting him hard on the back with his fists. Tim was kicking his legs, trying to get up on his knees, reaching around for a rock or a bush to pull against. Clouds of dust and pebbles made it hard for Mouse to see, but suddenly they began to roll again, this time closer to the edge of the cliff.

"Look out! The edge!" Mouse shouted again. She couldn't tell whether they heard her or not, but they stopped rolling. The light-haired boy leaped backward, and threw the shirt at Tim's head. He snatched up the gull and scooted away along the edge of the cliff. Then by mistake Mouse looked down at the feathery treetops, and had to close her eyes again.

When she opened them, the boy and the sea gull had disappeared, and Tim was getting gingerly to his feet and coming across the rocks toward her, his shirt hanging in ribbons from his hand.

"Wow," Mouse said. "What was *that* all about?"

"I don't know," Tim said in a furious, tight voice. Mouse could see that he was nearly crying with rage. "The first thing I knew he was on top of me, shouting something about leaving his bird alone." By now Tim had realized he was all right, and was walking around in a circle, kicking pebbles and getting his breath.

"*His* bird?"

"That's what he said. Come on, let's find him."

"Right."

They scrambled down the cliff and hurled themselves through the palm trees. Instinctively they split up, reaching the beach from separate angles. It was empty. There was no sign of the boy, or the sea gull.

Behind the beach the land rose, and Tim pointed to a path that slanted across the hillside. "Maybe it goes to that house we saw."

"It might." Mouse panted. "I'll try it."

"I'll go look past the cliff," Tim said.

"Okay."

Mouse tried to run, but the path's footing was rock shale, and she found herself slipping and sliding along through thick tropical bushes. Finally the path came out at an open field, where it wound through dry grass. On the other side of the field was a garden wall. The house was beyond.

It seemed quiet, dozing under its Spanish tile roof. Then a huge dog came running out barking, and Mouse heard an indifferent adult voice call the dog back. She backed off, nervous. The place seemed too sleepy to be hiding an active boy, and the dog was terrifying.

"He can't have come this far, anyway," she said to herself.

She pressed against the wall until the barking stopped, and then went back to the palm trees. Tim came back at almost the same time. There was no need to say anything. The boy was gone.

"We might as well eat lunch," Mouse said.

"Yeah," Tim said.

He brightened when they unpacked the picnic basket and found enough food for four people. They sat under the palms, chewing on chicken and devilled eggs and potato salad, fruit, and cupcakes. When they had stuffed themselves they lay in the shade beside the little tidal pool.

"But who do you suppose he was?" Mouse said. She lay on her side, trying to get her whole arm deep enough into the water to pick up a red stone from the bottom.

"You can't reach it. It only looks shallow because the water's so clear," Tim said. "I don't know. But I think he was the same boy who had the boat. I recognized his hair. Anyway" — a spider had run up Tim's leg and he stopped to flip it off — "you ought to have warned me when you saw him."

"But I didn't see him until you were fighting," Mouse said. She didn't want to say she had her eyes closed. "Was he strong?"

"He jumped me from behind, so I couldn't really tell. Anyone's stronger that way." Tim was still upset, mostly embarrassed that a strange boy had surprised and jumped him with such ease.

Mouse reached in for a banana.

"Hey, that's the last one."

"You can have half." She lay on her back, rubbing her knee with her toe. "If he said that was his bird, maybe he thought we were going to hurt it."

"How could he? Nobody hurts sea gulls,

and anyway he didn't even wait to see what we were going to do."

"Pygmies don't." Mouse stood up and started shinnying up a palm tree.

"Pygmies don't what."

"Stop to see." She found no foothold, and got down again. "Did you see how sunburned he was? And that light hair? I'm sure he's a pygmy."

"Whoever heard of a pygmy with white hair?"

"Down here they probably have different kinds."

Tim finished eating. "You make me sick. Can't you think of anything to talk about but pygmies?"

"Of course. But only when I feel like it." She was getting tired of the subject herself, and got out of it by starting to pack up the basket. "We might as well go. We've looked everywhere we can think of, and it must be getting late.

Tim got up. "Tomorrow let's rent the bikes Dad talked about. We can come this way on the road, and look some more."

"Okay."

Without warning Mouse felt like running, from the sunshine and the day and the good lunch. She leaped to her feet and rushed past Tim, down to the water where it was shallow, and turned up the beach. In a flash he shot by her, but she ran on, harder and harder until the water flew in sheets from her flying feet and the sun burned her shoulders. Then she got out of breath and had to stop. She flopped to the sand.

Tim came back. His face was dripping and he threw himself down. "Swim," he said.

"Just a sec. I can't breathe."

"There go the sea gulls." Tim looked up as the birds flew overhead, still mewing. "Darn," he said. "That was my favourite shirt." He picked up a shell and skipped it out to sea. "There's one thing I know, though."

"What?" Mouse's tone was cheerful as she started off again.

Tim turned around and looked at her, his blue eyes darkening. "I'm going to find that boy and get back at him, if it's the last thing I ever do."

Three

"Well," Mouse said, "what about Captain Fisher? He knows everybody around here, especially with boats. He might know where he lives."

"Good idea," Tim said. "We can ask as soon as we get there. But don't say what happened on the cliff."

It was six o'clock, and they were sitting on the wall in front of the hotel, wearing clean clothes and feeling hot and itchy. Their parents, delayed at the office, had arranged for a taxi to take them to Captain Fisher's house.

Mouse fidgeted with her hair. "You know, he must live somewhere near. That's twice in two days we've seen him."

"Yeah." Tim saw the taxi pulling around the hotel driveway and stood up. "We should keep an eye out now, too."

He had hoped they would be going in the direction of the cliff, but the taxi took the road along the water toward town. Tim and

Mouse hung out the windows, watching the bay. It looked cool and inviting in the late afternoon, but there was no sign of a small blue-and-white sloop on its broad expanse.

Halfway to town the driver turned inland, on a road that wound into the hills rising behind the bay. Forests of nutmeg trees and groves of limes blocked the view, and grew so high over the road that it was difficult seeing even the sky. Soon the car turned into a long driveway that led to a large house, surrounded by more trees and gardens. It pulled up in front and Mouse got out, feeling silly because the driver was holding the car door open for her. She thought how surprised he would be if she suddenly emerged through the window instead.

Mrs. Randolph came rushing out. "I didn't realize," she said. "There're other people here. It's not just us."

"It's all right," Mouse said. "We don't mind. We can eat."

"Oh, no." Tim grinned. "Hours of torture. We'll have to talk to everybody."

He was right. They were being propelled into a room full of grown people. Dad took them to each one, Captain Fisher first, and they shook hands politely and said yes, they loved the Caribbean, and it was the first time they had been in the tropics. After that Dad led them to the food table, and left.

"Umn, not bad," Tim said, munching a tart made with fruit. "It's got a funny taste, but good."

Mouse liked the coconut crisps, and filled her plate. Suddenly Tim nudged her in the ribs. "There's Captain Fisher. Come on."

Their father's friend was standing in another corner talking to several people, and Mouse and Tim edged up nearby until he saw them. He waved and came over, a tall, stalwart man who reminded Mouse of John Wayne.

"Doing all right?" he said.

"It's a very nice party," Tim said. He looked around for a place to put down his third fruit tart, and finally put it in his mouth.

"Have another," Captain Fisher said.

"No, thank you." Tim felt as though he were going to burst.

"I had a word with your father," Captain Fisher said. "In another week or two the fishing will ease up and I'll have a spare man. We'll take you out with the divers."

"That'd be great," Tim said. "We've been asking Dad about renting a boat of our own, too."

"I'd wait a while for that," Captain Fisher said. "Going off on your own isn't always the smartest thing to do, in a boat. Wait till you've learned a bit more."

Mouse put her plate down. "By the way, do you know a boy with white hair?"

"With a sloop, maybe," Tim added.

Captain Fisher looked at them. "A boy, with white hair?"

"Well, it's light yellow, then."

"And a sloop. Hmnnn." The man thought a minute. "Yes, it could be the same one."

"You've seen him?" Tim asked eagerly.

"I think so. Why?"

Tim blinked. "We were just wondering who he was. We saw him today."

"Well," Captain Fisher said. "If it's the same lad, sloop's blue, about twenty-odd feet or so."

They nodded.

"But I don't know him. Probably visiting somewhere along the coast. Seems to me I've seen his boat over in the eastern side of the bay."

"He must be a really good sailor," Tim said, "if he's out alone."

Captain Fisher looked at him shrewdly. "Could be. Or could be he's a fool." His face crinkled, and Mouse realized he was smiling. "But he's probably all right. Have to be, to handle that sloop."

A man came up to ask about the price of chartering a motor launch, and took Captain Fisher away.

"I like him," Mouse said.

"Me too," Tim said. "And now we know. It *is* the same boy."

"All we've got to do is find out where he lives."

"Yeah," Tim said. "And then how to get at him."

"Maybe Captain Fisher'll help us," Mouse said. "We don't have to tell him all of it, just say there aren't any other kids around here."

"Yes, but if Captain Fisher mentions us, the kid'll know," Tim said.

"Well, what about getting Captain Fisher to tell him he's got an emergency over here, or something." She shook her head. "No, that's dumb."

"Anyway, grown people never agree to do things like that," Tim said.

"Right." Mouse was thinking. "But a grown person might, just might" — her voice rose as her idea grew — "take him a message! We could make it fake, but something that would get him here. If we seal the envelope, I don't think Captain Fisher would read it."

"Okay. That's good. Let's figure out what to say."

It took a while to decide, sitting on an empty back terrace, but finally they wrote a message on a piece of paper from Captain Fisher's library. Then they went back to the party, and waited until Captain Fisher finished telling jokes to a group of guests. When they told him their plan, he fell neatly in with it.

"So you want to meet that boy, eh? Don't blame you, he's got a nice boat. Well, I can't guarantee anything, but I don't mind giving it a try. Going up the east coast in the morning, as a matter of fact."

"Thanks." Tim reached in his pocket and drew out the sealed envelope. "Just give him this." Mouse was already edging away. There was no point in getting asked more questions. "Can we call you tomorrow afternoon to see if you found him?"

"Sure."

"Okay, thanks," Tim said. "There's Mom. I think she wants us."

"Where's Mom?" whispered Mouse. "I don't see her."

"I just said that," Tim answered. "Let's go get something to drink."

"I want some more coconut crisps," Mouse said.

"Pig. You'll be sick."

Mouse often thought she could eat more than she really could, and was sick at embarrassing times as a result. Now she thought perhaps Tim was right and looked longingly at the plates of food but decided against any more.

"What'll we do now?" she said. If they weren't going to eat more, there didn't seem to be anything else to do.

"Well, we could find Dad and Mom and see if we're leaving soon. Or we could go outside." He pointed through a door into the garden.

The garden was full of interesting paths, and when they returned to the house they found Dad and Mom nearly the last people at the party, having a serious conversation with a group of guests. Mom looked disturbed and Mouse wondered what it was. She heard one of the men saying he was sorry, but there was nothing he could do.

"Well, it looks like that settles it," they heard Dad say.

"What a shame," Mom added.

Later, in the backseat of the car riding down the mountain through the nutmeg groves, Tim asked, "Is anything wrong?"

"Yes," Mom said. "We're having some problems. The price of minerals has gone up all over the world, and the bauxite on these islands is no exception, I guess. It's what happened with oil in the Middle East, although that was for a different reason."

"What'll you do?" Mouse said.

"We don't know yet," Dad answered. "We'll have to talk to the Chicago office, plus try to find a solution here. But it doesn't look good."

"Things always look gloomier late at night, dear." Mom touched his arm lightly. She turned to Mouse and Tim. "Did you have a good time?"

"Yes," Tim said. "It turned out to be a big success."

"Umn," Mouse added. She felt sleepy, and she stared out of the window. First she closed one eye, then the other, trying to tell which one could see better.

"Pssst." Tim interrupted her experiments in a low voice. "Do you think he'll come?"

"I hope so," Mouse whispered. She turned back to the window, but it was getting too dark to see much, and she thought about the boy with white hair. Could he really be a pygmy? No, of course not, that was too silly, but there *was* something mysterious about him. Suppose he wasn't really a boy, but a wild creature who had come out of the sea, living like the birds and the wind, racing his boat across the broad sweeps of the Caribbean Sea with only the squeak of his sails and the sunsets and dawns for his company.

"Then," she decided, without knowing why, "I wish I was him."

That night there was a sudden summer rain. Rolf had left his mat on deck to sleep below in the bunk, and the dawn swell woke him. For a minute he was confused in the dark cabin, for he was used to waking on deck. But then he saw the open hatch above him, and standing on the bunk, caught hold of the edges of the hatch and jumped. He hooked his elbows over and hung looking out, his legs swinging.

He saw Zec perched on the boom, his head still under his wing. He watched a pelican swoop down through the dawn mist to the gray water and catch a fish. The fish flapped hard for a minute, buffeting the pelican's big beak, and still moved when it was inside the pouch. Then the pelican flew too far away for Rolf to see it, and he lowered his feet to the bunk and jumped again. This time he made it to the deck.

The boy sat down in the bow to wait for the sun. The sky was very light over the mountains to the east, and then suddenly the sun broke the mist, throwing purple-black clouds all over the sky, which turned blue. The water turned blue, too, as the sun flicked the surface, and Rolf could see the bottom. Now he could swim. Barracuda never stayed in the bay after sunrise.

He turned around and saw that Zec had waked up. The gull was sleepily mewing, edging along the boom. Rolf threw him a piece of fish from a bucket on the deck.

He went out on the bowsprit and eased into the water. It was almost cold, not yet warmed by the day's heat, and Rolf felt empty and heavy at first until his strong strokes made the blood flow. He watched the nearby beach, the sun shooting green-gold haze through the trees, and then he put his head down and swam the rest of the way underwater. He opened his eyes and saw the dim green and the white of the sandy bottom below. When he broke the surface he was at the beach, and he splashed ashore noisily, singing.

Rolf had a knife in his belt, and he walked

to an inlet where some mangrove trees grew in the water. He pulled up some of the root branches, cutting them off. They were covered with small oysters, about eight to a branch, and when he had five or six sticks covered with the green barnacled shells he swam back to the boat.

He climbed dripping to the deck, and Zec hopped down, waiting eagerly while Rolf pried open the shells and dug out the juicy meat. He threw the gull all it could eat, and then put his own in a tin cup and sat down on the cabin top to have his breakfast.

While he was eating he heard a faint chugging, and looked up. "Captain Fisher, Zec," he said. The water from his bathing suit ran down on the deck in little dribbles as he peered toward the west. In a minute he saw a motor launch moving slowly in the bay. It left a rippled wake that caught the sunlight.

"Wonder what they're doing out so early," Rolf said, resuming his eating.

The sea gull hopped down beside him again, and Rolf put a final oyster in the open beak and laughed.

"You've had enough. Go catch yourself some fish."

The chugging grew nearer. Rolf set down

his cup and watched the launch, narrow-eyed.

"What do they want over here?" he muttered, suddenly angry that anyone could trespass in his cove. People rarely came this close in to shore along here and the coast road turned inland before it got this far. But still, if anyone wanted to look, here he was. Now the launch was near enough for him to see the men moving on deck, coiling ropes and stacking the diving gear.

Rolf leaned forward tensely, scarcely breathing, knowing with a sudden sinking feeling that the launch was coming directly toward him. He thought wildly of throwing up the sails and trying to outrun them, but even as the thought flashed through his mind he knew he was too late. By the time he got underway the launch would be on him.

No, he would have to stay where he was and figure out a plan of escape after he saw what they were going to do. He slid along the cabin top, waiting, his hand unthinkingly going to the knife at his belt.

"Here they come, Zec," he whispered, for the sea gull too was watching from its perch on the jib, turning its head from side to side.

The big launch cut its motor and glided, coming into the still water of the little cove.

For a minute there was a deadly silence.

Rolf crouched without moving, and then a distant hail came across the water.

"Sloop, hey-y-y," and Rolf saw the tall figure of Captain Fisher on the foredeck. He waited. He would never answer, no matter what they did.

"They know we're here. Now let them come and get us, Zec," he said quietly, his fists tightening.

The launch came closer, and Rolf could see the men watch him curiously. Captain Fisher was standing calmly with a coil of rope in his hand. Then the rope snaked through the air and landed with a thump on the *Windsong*'s deck.

"Make it fast." Captain Fisher's voice was surprisingly cheerful. "And be quick."

For a minute Rolf stared at him, and then he leaned forward and looped the rope over his deck stanchion. Whatever they planned to do, now was no time to make a break. Better to have open water, where he at least had a chance.

Involuntarily his lips tightened, and he braced himself. But the men on board the launch made no further move, and Captain Fisher left the foredeck and came along the rail.

"Hey, you, boy," he shouted.

Rolf didn't answer, but waited calmly.

"I've got something for you. A message." Captain Fisher seemed unperturbed by his cool reception.

Rolf left the bow and walked amidships. "What is it?" he said, and in the early morning stillness his voice carried clearly.

"Just this. Catch." Captain Fisher stepped to the rail of his boat, and Rolf saw his arm jerk out and back, and heard the thump of a heavy object land on the *Windsong*'s forward deck. Then the launch's motor came alive with a sputter, and she began to backwater. The rope dropped. It was moving away. They were leaving!

Rolf stood watching silently until he saw the Captain wave his hand in farewell, and then he went forward and picked up the packet on the deck.

"What in the world . . ." he said to Zec, who had retired from the strangers inside a coil of rope. "It's a message. Well, I'm not going to read it."

But as he went to the rail to throw it over, he hesitated. After all, it wouldn't do any harm to see what it said. It might be something he should know.

He unwrapped the oilskin and spread out a

piece of paper. He read the message once, then stood scratching his head. It wasn't from home as he expected, but from someone who signed himself "The Chief."

"Who . . .," Rolf said, and then, "Of course. The cliff."

"If you want a fair fight," the message read, "come again to the cliff rocks. Tonight at the moon's height. Otherwise I will know that the white-haired boy fights only from behind."

Rolf turned to the sea gull and grinned, his white teeth flashing in his sunburned face. "What do you think, Zec? Should we go see what this is all about?"

"How old do you think he is?" Mouse asked, watching Tim try to comb his hair. It was stiff from three days in the sun and salt water, even though he kept wetting it to make it flat.

"I don't know. Around my age." Tim held out a brown arm and bulged up his muscle. "I hope I can beat him."

"You've got to," Mouse said. "Otherwise you'll make us look like idiots."

It was late afternoon, and they were in their room at the hotel, getting dressed early for dinner. All morning they had played tennis, and after lunch they had ridden bicycles to town. They had hung around Captain Fisher's docks, waiting for the boats to come in. Finally the big lead launch chugged into sight, and Captain Fisher waved from its cockpit.

"Message delivered!" he shouted.

"Great!" Tim shouted back. "Thanks!"

To their relief Captain Fisher had only waved again and then turned back to his work.

"No questions," Tim said. "That's good."

"Now all we need to do is find out what time the height of the moon is," Mouse said.

"Let's try the pharmacy," Tim said. "They know stuff like that."

But the pharmacist had directed them instead to the town newspaper office, where, he said, they could find a tide table that listed sunrise and moonrise.

"We have to figure halfway in between," Mouse said, as they pedalled rapidly toward the hotel, with the local paper sticking out of her shorts. "And that's got to be the right time."

They had put away their bikes and sat on a wall to read the paper. It said that moonrise would be at nine, and moonset would be at three A.M. "That means it'll be highest at midnight."

"Perfect." Mouse jumped up. "Let's go upstairs and plan."

Now, Tim gave up on his hair and started digging for a shirt. "You know, there's no good way to get out of our rooms at night without being seen," he said. "People around here stay up late."

"We should get a rowboat, and anchor it in the water," Mouse volunteered. "We could drop down with huge beach umbrellas and leave."

"Don't be dumb. This is serious."

"Well, we could get out from the second floor," she said. "There's that little terrace under the window at the end of the hall. I don't think it's used very much. That end's closest to the rocks, too."

"We could break our legs. It's a good twenty-foot drop," Tim said. "But we might make it with a rope."

While Mouse changed, he went down the hall to look.

"It's okay," he announced when he came back. He had to shout because Mouse had gone in the bathroom to wash and the water was running. "And we'd better wear our pa-

jamas over our clothes," he called, "so if anyone sees us they'll never suspect anything."

Mouse came out of the bathroom. She went
on the balcony of their room and hung pre-
cariously over the rail. "What time do you
think we should leave?" she said.

"Probably about ten." Tim was struggling
into his shoes. "I wish we never had to wear
shoes," he said.

"If we either had to wear them all the time
or not at all, it would be better," Mouse
agreed. She ran her fingers along the balcony
railing. It was dark wood and there were some
kind of bugs that lived in it. That morning
she had tried to lure them out with bread
crumbs, but they seemed not hungry and
wouldn't come.

"Never wear them." Tim stood up and
rushed out on the balcony, flailing his fists in
short punching jabs. "That, and that! I'll get
you, you . . ."

Mouse giggled. "You look so silly." Her tone
grew serious. "I wish Mom would let us drink
coffee. It's going to be hard to stay awake."

"If we did, she'd know something was
funny." Tim threw himself on the long couch
at one end of the balcony. "I'm going to learn

yoga. Some guy at school stood on his head for an hour last spring."

He got on his shoulders and then up on his head, jamming his feet against the wall when he wavered. Suddenly he saw his watch and came down and jumped to his feet. His combed hair was standing up again. "Gosh, dinner's in ten minutes. I'd better go ask around and get some rope. You find Mom and Dad, and I'll meet you in the dining room."

"Don't let anybody see you," Mouse said.

Tim laughed and shut the door quietly behind him, and Mouse looked off again across the bay. In the west the mountains were shot with sunset light, and blue clouds hung down to touch them. She felt so good she shivered, and hugged herself with her arms. She wondered what the white-haired boy had done when he got the message. Was he excited? Did he want to meet them, too? Well, she thought, if he comes, it won't be long before we find out.

The dinner gong rang and she turned indoors.

Four

Tim looked at his watch. It was ten minutes after eleven. He was standing on the little terrace, and above him Mouse hung over the windowsill, reaching down the rope with her hand.

"Hold it tighter," she called. "It's floppy."

"I'm trying," he hissed. "Just get going. I can't hang on all day."

She heaved herself over and swung, dropping hand over hand. The rope swayed and her hand slipped. She let go and dropped with a yelp.

"Shut up!" Tim said.

"Shut up yourself." She scrambled to her feet. "I was scared."

"It was worth it," he said. "We're out. Come on."

They hurried into the hotel garden, the grass wet on their bare feet. The garden was black and mysterious and full of flower smells. They pushed their way through the bushes, away from the lights and clatter of the hotel, until they reached the wall above the beach. They stopped to hide their pajamas in the bushes and put on their tennis shoes, which were tied by the laces around their waists.

The night was breathless and heavy, as summer was the restless season of bright heat and sudden evening rains. Clouds drifted across the sky, regularly blotting out the moon, and the wall was a black blob before the deeper black beach. Mouse began to wonder if she really wanted to do this. The big rocks at the end of the beach looked terrifying in the dim light from their flashlights, and she could tell that Tim was hesitating too.

"We never thought about no moon," she said.

"It'll probably come out again," he answered. "But I think we should go inland."

They slipped and slid through the undergrowth, and clambered over boulders on the hill behind the beach until they were past the point of rocks. A faint track opened ahead, leading down to the water again. Tiny waves made little slapping noises on the sand, and the warm night air was soft. Mouse began to relax. The rest of the walk along the beach was easy, and in fifteen minutes they were at the base of the cliff.

Tim pointed his flashlight up to pick out a climbing route. He could hear the low soughing of a swelling tide, and he hoped there wasn't a strong current around the point. He wondered how a boat could find her way in to the beach in such darkness without smashing herself to bits on the underwater rocks that guarded all the beaches. But then, he reflected, the white-haired boy probably knew how to do it, if he had been here long. Tim jammed the flashlight in his back pocket and started climbing.

Behind him, Mouse shuddered as the breeze hit the cliff and turned into a sinister whine. The darkness gave her dismal thoughts and she wondered if Captain Fisher had really found the right boy, and if the boy could read. People who lived in the wilds never bothered with school — they probably had never even heard of it.

Then she looked up, and to her joy saw that the clouds were parting. The moon was coming out after all! Immediately she felt better. "He'll come," she decided. "He's bound to. Nobody could ignore a note like ours, unless he's a creep."

"Hurry up!" It was Tim, above her. She could see him plainly now, standing up beckoning. She went higher, and partly crouching and partly crawling on her hands and knees, scrabbled up toward him, taking care to keep low. They didn't want any silhouette showing above the cliff.

At the top, Mouse stopped and caught her breath. Yesterday they had not come this high, and now, for the first time, she could see to the west, all the way to the other side of the bay. It was beautiful, with the moon dropping a trembling path on the water and the clouds reflecting light above the mountains. Far out, by the reef, she saw some small islands, round and flat like pancakes. Closer, she saw the bright lights of the town, with its houses strung along the shore like twinkling candles.

Tim stirred restlessly.

"What's the matter?" Mouse asked, twisting around to look at him.

"I wish he'd hurry. And I hope he's willing to really fight." Tim wiggled his toes. His sneakers were full of sand, and he leaned over to empty them. When he straightened up again, he saw something moving, far out. It was a boat. He put his hand on Mouse's shoulder.

"Look." He pointed.

She saw it too, cutting through the water. "It's him," she said.

"It might not be. There might be other boats that size."

"But they wouldn't be out now, would they?" Mouse said.

"Probably not."

They watched the boat come steadily nearer. It was coming on a straight beat across the bay. Slowly its details took shape in the moonlight, and its blurred outlines became clearer. It *was* a small sloop. Tim felt a tightening feeling in his stomach.

"The moon is right in the middle of the sky," Mouse said. "At its height."

Tim didn't answer, and Mouse realized he was shivering.

"Are you afraid?" she whispered.

"No, just excited."

The boat had stopped. It was some distance, still, from the beach, but the sails were coming down and they could see a figure, with tiny sticks for arms and legs, moving around on the deck. Then there was a faint movement and a rippled trail through the water toward the shore.

"He's swimming in," Tim said.

Just then the moon went behind another cloud. The sudden dark made them draw closer together. "Now we won't know when he gets here," Mouse said.

"Yes, we will, we'll hear him coming up the cliff. The rocks will rattle."

"We better split up. Where shall I be?"

"Over there," Tim said. "But not too far."

She touched his arm, embarrassed, and then worked her way backward across the top and sat down with her back against a rock. For a few minutes there was no sound except the water below, rumbling gently at the foot of the cliff, and the darkness seemed to grow blacker. Suddenly Mouse thought of spiders, and sat bolt upright. There was no telling where they lived in the tropics. Probably in the bushes, she thought, not up here. It's too high.

She sat back down again and her back itched, but she decided not to scratch. The boy must be near by now and he might hear her, or see her move. As the moon came closer to the edge of the cloud, there was a dim light. Then suddenly she saw him. He was standing up on the top, right on a level with Tim.

Tim saw him too, and moved out from his hiding place.

Mouse could see the two figures begin to walk toward each other, slipping on the poor footing. They came almost together, and stopped. Mouse thought, now it's coming. She held her breath. Blood pounded in her head, and the wind and the moonlight, bright now, seemed to fill the sky.

Tim began to wave, and she stood up to see better. He must be waving in furious anger. Chills shot up her back. Then she heard him call her.

"Mouse, Mouse, come here!" he shouted, his voice made distant by the wind.

She scrambled to her feet and rushed forward, slipping and sliding over the unseen crevices. A rustling noise slid away to her right and she squeaked with fear, but she kept on, and in a minute she reached them.

Tim was smiling.

"Why don't you fight him?" Mouse demanded.

"He doesn't want to. He says it was his pet sea gull I was trying to rescue, but he thought I was going to hurt it. That's why he jumped on me." Tim turned to the boy, who was standing very still.

"Oh." Mouse was disappointed, but a fight was out of the question. She looked more closely at the white-haired boy, and saw that he was not quite as tall as Tim, but he looked muscular. His hair did indeed look white, made even more so by the bright moonlight.

"What's your name?" Mouse asked.

"Rolf."

"Ralph?"

"No, R-O-L-F," he spelled it out. "It's Danish."

"Oh, I know. Like *Beowulf*. We had it in school."

"Beowulf was a Viking, stupid," Tim said.

"What are your names?" Rolf interrupted.

They told him, and he was quiet for a minute, looking around. "I was worried when you sent me that note. Is anybody else with you?"

"No. Why?"

"Nothing." Rolf sat down, and they saw a knife flash in the belt of his trunks. "Well, what should we do now?"

"We could have a picnic," Mouse said. "That's what we were doing the other day when we decided to climb the cliff and saw your bird."

"We haven't got any food," Tim said.

"I do," Rolf said.

They looked at him.

"On my boat," he said. "Would you like to come down?"

"That's a great idea," Tim said.

"Yes." Mouse agreed.

Rolf led them down the cliff by a different way. It was much faster, and in a few minutes they stood on the sand. Mouse looked around. "I like this beach," she said.

"I come here to swim sometimes at night," Rolf said. "It's one of the few places the barracuda don't come in."

Tim looked at this boy and wondered who he was that he could swim at night with no one to stop him. But he said nothing, and they began to walk along the beach.

"You'll have to swim," Rolf said, when they came opposite the anchored sloop. "I never thought I'd be bringing you back. I mean, I didn't know what you wanted, or who you were, but I thought you were enemies."

"We thought so too," Mouse said.

Rolf plunged in, with Tim right beside him. Mouse tried not to think about what might be in the dark water under her stomach or just behind her feet. She kept her eyes on the two heads in front of her, and swam as fast as she could. They came to the anchor line first, and then the gleaming white bow loomed overhead. Rolf swam farther out, around the sloop's stern, until he reached a little rope ladder. He put one hand up to steady it. "There's a wire rail at the top," he said.

Mouse swung up the ladder and under the cable railing, and found herself on a shiny wooden deck. The boys followed, puddles dripping from their legs. Rolf reached into the cockpit for towels.

"The food's below," he said. He led the way down a ladder into the cabin and turned on a lamp. Mouse and Tim stared. It was perfect. A bunk fitted against one side, under built-in shelves and a tiny porthole. Against the other side was a tiny gallery, and an icebox. Another tiny porthole opened above a little table. The forward end of the cabin held built-in chests made of dark glowing mahogany. They could see a water basin, and even a tiny toilet. Everything gleamed with wood and brass in the flickering light.

"How long have you had this boat?" Tim said. "It's fantastic."

"I got it last year," Rolf said, and Mouse thought she saw his expression darken. "My father gave it to me for my birthday. Her name is *Windsong*."

"That's a perfect name," Mouse said.

Rolf dug in a cupboard and got out peanut butter and some bread, and three Pepsis. They followed him up the companionway to the deck and sat down in the moonlight on the cabin top.

Mouse heard a queer noise, and then she

realized it was Rolf's sea gull perched on the boom.

"Where did you get him?" she asked.

"We found him, when he was so young he could hardly fly," Rolf answered. "Somehow he had hurt himself, and he never got really strong. Even now he can't fly very long at a time."

"Oh." Mouse thought of being a sea gull, born to the wind and sky, and not being able to fly very long at a time.

"He's happy, anyway, I think," Rolf said, and she wondered if the boy had read her thoughts. But he was standing up, moving forward to the bowsprit.

"What's his name?" Tim followed.

"Zec. It's a Mexican name." Rolf sat with his feet propped on the bobstays. His body moved easily with the bobbing motion of the boat, and Mouse thought he looked as though he had been born there.

"Are you from here?" she asked.

"No. Not this island, anyway." He stuffed the rest of his sandwich in his mouth and suddenly swung down, like a monkey, into the water. His light hair made a white blob when he dived under. Mouse looked at Tim, who shook his head. Rolf came up and treaded water.

"Where're *you* from?" he called.

"Chicago," Tim answered.

"No, I meant around here."

"The hotel. We've come for the summer."

"How did you know Captain Fisher?" Rolf leaned back and floated, moving his arms back and forth in the water. "And what made you think he knew me?"

"He doesn't know you. But he said he'd seen your boat around, and he thought he could find it," Tim said.

"He's a friend of our father's," Mouse added. "They've known each other for a long time."

Rolf climbed up the ladder and stood on the deck beside Tim. Mouse wondered idly who would have won if he and Tim had fought. This way was better, she decided. If they'd fought, she and Tim would never have come to the boat.

"You see, our parents are working here," Tim was explaining. Rolf sat down, listening carefully. When Tim finished, Rolf nodded.

"I'm not surprised they're having trouble on this island," he said.

"What do you mean?"

"Because my father always said it was a very political island," Rolf answered.

"I wish your father could explain that to Dad," Mouse said. "Dad's really upset."

Rolf stood up. "No." Something in his voice made her stop talking, and she got up too.

Tim changed the subject. "I really like your boat," he said. "What size is it? I mean, how long?" He started picking up the peanut butter and the Pepsi cans.

"Twenty-four feet," Rolf said. "A good size to handle."

"I wish I knew how to sail," Tim said.

Rolf was quiet for a moment. Then he seemed to take a breath. "We could go sailing tomorrow if you want to, and I'll show you."

Tim put the cans down and smiled. "Hey, that'd be great."

Mouse leaned over the rail. Whatever the tension was, it had passed, and she felt light with relief. "We could go away and never come back," she said.

"No, we couldn't," Tim said. "Dad would have a fit." He turned to Rolf. "He'll have a fit if he finds out we're not in the hotel, too. I think we better get back."

"Okay, I'll show you the cliff path," Rolf said. He slid off the deck and into the water, like a shining light seal.

"This has been really fun," Mouse said. On a sudden impulse, she lowered herself backward from the rail and hung by her knees. She let go and fell in with a splash.

Tim climbed on the bowsprit again, balancing for a last look.

"I can't wait till tomorrow," he said, almost to himself. Then he dived into the water, and followed the others ashore.

Five

At breakfast Mom and Dad were busy talking about the office, and at first Mouse and Tim's silence went unnoticed.

"Are you going to do something interesting today?" Dad asked suddenly.

"What?" Mouse said. She smothered a yawn, and Mom looked at her narrowly.

"Maybe you should go to bed earlier."

"Mom."

"Well-l-l . . ." Mom was watching Dad pour the coffee. "That's enough, thank you. We'll see. I don't want you getting run down."

"Mom, that is the dumbest thing to say," Mouse began indignantly. But Tim kicked her under the table, and she picked up her orange juice. "I feel fine," she finished meekly.

Tim changed the subject. "Dad, what does it mean when people say this is a political island?"

"It means that people here care about politics," Dad said. "There are seventeen island groups, including this one, in the West Indies. Many of them used to belong to European countries like France, Holland, England, or Denmark. Now that they're independent, they're very serious about their new governments."

Mr. Randolph pushed back his chair. "Politics touches everyone here, and elections rouse strong feelings."

"One of the big issues here is what to do with the island's natural resources," Mom added. "There's going to be an election next month. One candidate wants to sell bauxite to other countries, like the United States. The other candidate wants to keep everything right here. That's why it's a bit uncertain for our company. Dad and I could be talking to people who may not be in power next autumn."

"What're you going to do in the meantime?" Mouse asked.

"Wait, or look elsewhere. We haven't made up our minds," her mother said. She pushed back her sunglasses. "But that doesn't have to affect your fun. Now, as Dad said, what're your plans for today?"

"We're going to fool around in the water," Tim said.

* * *

"I felt really guilty when you told them that," Mouse said when she and Tim were back in their room. "I'm not sure we should go with Rolf now."

"I know. But I think this one time is okay. Then if Rolf asks us again, we'll tell Mom and Dad." Tim finished stuffing his things in a canvas bag. "If we'd said anything now, there could be a big flap over nothing. I mean, I'm sure Rolf'll come, but suppose he doesn't show up, or something?"

"Or suppose it's a trick, to get us in his mercy," Mouse said. "Last night could have been just to lull our suspicions."

"We could still have that fight then." Tim grinned and opened the door.

"You know, I think Rolf's keeping something back," Mouse said.

"I know. But I like him anyway."

"I do too. What do you suppose it is?"

"I don't know, but I don't think it's anything in his personality. It's something that's happened."

"You're right," Mouse said, surprised. She hadn't thought of that. She smiled at the man at the front desk as he handed her their lunch bag. They went out up the beach in the bright, sparkly morning, and it seemed hard to believe that anything could happen to anyone in such a marvellous place. When they reached the top of the cliff, the *Windsong* was in the cove.

"He *did* come," Tim said, starting down. "Hurry. I see him on deck."

They hailed the sloop from the beach, and swam out at Rolf's wave, holding the lunch in the air with the canvas bag. Zec greeted them with flapping wings and a hiss, and Rolf took the food and stowed it in the cabin. Then he stood and looked at them, smiling.

"Do you still want to learn to sail?" he asked.

"Of course," Tim said.

Rolf looked at the sky. The clouds were high up and racing, meaning a breeze farther out in the bay. "Do you think you'll get seasick?"

"No." Tim was determined not to let this boy, who could do everything well, outdo him in that department. Tim never got sick.

"I hope not," Mouse said. "But if I do, I won't care."

Rolf laughed and led them to the back of the boat. "Okay. This end, behind the cabin, is called the stern, and the front's the bow. You probably know that."

"Right."

"And on a boat, the right side is called starboard. Left is port."

They nodded.

"There are different kinds of sailboats," Rolf went on. "There are yawls and ketches and schooners, which are usually bigger, longer boats. *Windsong*'s a sloop, with one mast."

He pointed at it, an aluminum shaft standing up from the cabin top. Then he walked forward and put his hand on a rope which ran down the mast and wound around a cleat. "On a boat all ropes are called lines. The line that's used to pull *up* a sail is called a halyard, and the line you used to pull *in* the sail is a sheet." He grinned. "Got all that?"

Mouse shook her head. "You will," he said. "All the names for things on boats are from the old sailing days of the big sailing clippers, but even now they make sense when you get used to them."

He moved up to the bow. "This boat has two sails. That big one that goes up the main mast is called the main. This smaller one running from the bow is called the jib."

"Jib booms and bobstays," Mouse said. "I've heard of that."

Tim shot her a withering glance. He thought he was going to like this. It seemed easy so far. Rolf moved carefully, and told everything very clearly. Now he was undoing the elastic ties that kept the mainsail rolled up along the boom. The sail drooped down, and Rolf pointed at the line he had shown Tim earlier, on the mast.

"Untie that," he said, "and haul it up."

Tim took the line and pulled, hand over hand, feeling a surge of excitement as the big mainsail rose steadily above him, light coloured against the blue sky. It slapped hard as it reached the top, and the *Windsong* began to tug restlessly on her anchor line. Rolf was in the cockpit, one hand on the tiller, the other loosening the main sheet.

"Now go forward," he told Tim. "And haul up the jib. The line's there on the mast — on the other side from the main halyard. Mouse, you can pull up the anchor. Now."

The anchor was heavier than Mouse expected, but by bracing herself she managed to get it up to the edge of the deck. There it stopped, too heavy for her to lift over.

Tim leaped to help, and together they got it, trailing seaweed, on deck. The boat turned slowly, while Rolf watched the mainsail. It swung out, and gradually filled with air. He pushed the tiller hard over, letting the main sheet run out through his fingers.

"I'm paying it out," Rolf said. "That means letting the sail go out far enough to catch the breeze and get us started."

The boat began to pick up speed, moving away from the beach. Her sails tightened, straining against the lines. They came out of the shelter of the cliff and the breeze shifted, coming from the right. The sloop heeled over in a sudden gust, and Tim and Mouse grabbed at the nearest handhold. Rolf balanced easily, his eyes still watching the sails. Now he brought the mainsail in, and pointed the bow to starboard. Behind them the hull left a creaming wake in the water, and overhead the sun shone down with a hot brilliance, reflecting in a million tiny gleams on the dark blue bay. The tame sea gull left the cabin and rose on the wind above their heads, floating there like a kite. After a few minutes he landed again, as gracefully as he had gone. He flapped once to steady himself, then settled back on the mast.

"I don't think I'm going to be sick at all," said Mouse.

"I think I'm going to spend the rest of my life on a boat," Tim said.

Rolf grinned. He stood up on the edge of the cockpit, one foot working the tiller. Tim and Mouse had to lean close to hear what he was saying.

"Okay. If the wind was from behind all the time, there'd be nothing to sailing. But the wind can be coming from any direction, and you may want to go a certain place, or stay in a channel. So the main thing is to figure out which way the wind's coming from, and work with it to get where you want to go."

"What do you do if the wind's coming from straight in front of you?" Mouse asked. "How do you keep from going backward?"

"You tack," Rolf said. "I'll show you that. But right now the wind's coming from starboard. We want to head across the bay. So, we'll point the bow away from the wind, loosen the sails, and go on a broad reach." He moved over. "One of you can try."

"Me, okay?" Tim looked at Mouse.

She nodded. "Sure, you'd die if you didn't."

In the instant that Tim caught hold of the tiller, he felt the powerful swing of the water under the boat. He pushed the tiller right, and the boat began to turn left. "Starboard and port," he reminded himself. Suddenly the boom came flying across the cockpit, narrowly missing their heads. Rolf grabbed the main sheet and the tiller, all at the same time. The boat turned back again and the sails filled on the other side.

"We were jibing," Rolf said. "You can capsize when you jibe, or tear out all the rigging. So I had to jump." He saw Tim's embarrassment. "I jibed a lot too, when I was learning. The sails lose their wind. I should have warned you. You have to keep her headed closer to the wind all the time. Now try again."

Tim took the tiller once more. He was nervous and the sloop's bow wobbled a little, but he held her on course, and Rolf looked pleased. "Now we'll try coming about," he said.

He took the tiller and pushed *Windsong*'s bow sharply around, and this time, as the boom swept across to the other side, the sails simply emptied and filled up again.

"I don't see the difference between that turn and the one I did," Tim said.

"You will, after you've sailed more," Rolf said.

"Do you ever use the motor?" Mouse asked.

Rolf shook his head. "Hardly ever. Outboards are for emergencies, really. Or maybe for getting out of a bad harbour, where the wind's not coming from the right direction and you've got to get out anyway. Then you'd lower the sail and use the outboard."

All morning they practiced, with the sun beating down on them, feeling swept through and cleaned by the wind and the salt water. Mouse learned as much from watching Tim as she did from her own turns, and she found that what Rolf had said was true — each time they switched places, the unfamiliar sailing terms became easier to remember. But still, she thought, they were weird names. Words like companionway for ladder, halyard for wire, and head for the little toilet.

Once she went and sat on the edge of the deck, dangling her feet. They were well out in the bay by now, where the waves rose in big hills and valleys of water. Mouse thought the wind was like a wall, pushing them, making the *Windsong* rise up on her side, or sometimes dip the deck into the water. When the boat fell across the troughs, Mouse's toes combed the surface, then rose again on the top of the sea. The spray flung across her, feeling cold and good on her hot face, tasting the salt.

The sun rose higher, hotter and hotter on their arms and legs and faces. They got hungry, and realized it was past noon. Rolf pointed ahead to the flat round islands Mouse had seen the night before, out near the reefs. "We can go ashore there, and swim and eat."

"Good idea."

Rolf took the tiller and guided the *Windsong* into a narrow channel between the reef on the outside and the islands to port. Columns of coral thrust up from the water, and Tim watched Rolf's hands move the tiller, now in a wide swing, now a barest movement. Over the side Mouse could see the rocks slip by, inches away, the water ahead running in a current, dark blue and cloudy, or pale and green.

"What about that island, close to the reef?"

"It's nothing but a wall of trees."

"Those are mangroves," Rolf said. "I think there's an opening."

He was right, and in a minute the *Windsong* prowled quietly into a little cove. She glided over the still, clear water toward an empty white beach, and Rolf gave Mouse the tiller. "Hold it steady," he said. He ran forward to be ready to lower the sails. Tim went up front, waiting with the anchor.

"Hold-d-d it," Rolf called. "Head up into the wind, hold it a minute more. *Now!*"

Tim flung the anchor. The boat kept going, reached the end of the anchor line and swung around. Rolf dropped the sails, and for a minute no one moved.

"Now we've got to furl them." Rolf's cheerful voice broke the silence. "Roll up, like this, and fold them in. Use the elastics."

When they finished Rolf dashed to the rail. "Last one in's a rotten egg," he said. He dived over, and they could see his body clearly all the way down to the bottom. When he came up they were in the water with him, splashing their way to the beach.

"Are there any more cookies?"

"Two."

"Oh."

"I don't want any more," Rolf said. "I'm stuffed. You eat them."

"Okay." Mouse put the cookies in her mouth.

They had feasted on the beach, tearing into the hotel's lunch — big hunks of chicken, tomatoes, hard-boiled eggs, and cookies. Rolf had found some mango fruit on a tree and they had eaten that too, all they could hold. Now they lay back on the beach, full, and Mouse picked out some thick slices of yellow cheese.

"We didn't eat this."

"I can't. Give it to Zec," Tim said. The sea gull was standing nearby on the sand.

"He won't eat it, he only likes fish." Rolf rolled over. Mouse lay on her back, and when the sun shone in her eyes she put a slice of cheese across her face.

"Gross," Tim said.

Mouse sat up, giggling. "It's melting."

Tim jumped to his feet and ran into the water. "Let's explore," he said.

"Do you think anybody lives here?" Mouse asked Rolf.

"I doubt it," he said. "I thought I saw a boat here the other day, but I'm not sure. We can look around, though."

Behind the beach was a shallow inlet, and they followed that, walking between palm trees in water up to their knees. Zec rode on Rolf's shoulder, but in a few minutes he began to make mewing noises. Suddenly he flew up in the air.

"He doesn't like to get too far from the beach," Rolf said, watching him go. "He's going back."

They came to a grove of coconut palms, and beyond that they could see a low hill rising out of a natural meadow.

"Let's climb it," Tim said.

He began to run, and they hurled themselves after him, the wind tearing their hair and the grass whipping their bare feet.

"Hi, wait." Mouse couldn't go any farther, and sank down to get her breath. The others didn't hear her and kept on. She could see it was a race and watched the two figures toiling up the slope of the hill. One stood on top, and she saw it was Tim. She wondered if Rolf would feel bad, and then decided not. He could do most things better than they. He'd been behind at the start anyway.

She lay back in the grass and turned over on her face. The ground smelled of sand and salt and grass, and other things she did not know. Then she laced her fingers over her eyes and looked at the sky, turning her head slowly around to see the whole horizon. Suddenly she stopped.

She saw something farther along on the right-hand slope of the hill, and took her hands away to get a better look. Her eyes had lights in them from the pressure of her fingers, and she blinked, trying to see. The sun's high glare reflected clearly on a greyish building that rose out of the grass, with clumps of bushes clustered at its base.

"What *is* that?" she muttered, and stood up. Rolf and Tim were coming back now, stumbling at a jog trot through the meadow. She ran toward them.

"Look." She pointed, and they turned.

"It's a ruined building."

"It's an old sugar mill," Rolf said. "Let's go see."

In a minute they stood looking up at its gray tower, with the vines curling up it. They could hear the wind whistling across the top.

"How long has it been here?"

"A hundred and fifty years probably," Rolf answered. "There used to be lots of big sugar mills on the main island. This little island might have been one whole sugar plantation."

"But why would they leave?"

"Pirates, anything. There were lots of revolutions, or maybe the soil got bad from a hurricane. Hurricanes wash salt over everything."

They went inside, and found themselves in a circular room. The floor was dirt, and just under the roof was what looked like an inside balcony.

Rolf eyed the walls. "Most of these mills have double walls. There should be some steps. Yes, there."

They went through a tiny doorway behind some rubble and found a narrow passageway with steps leading up. They came out on the balcony, which seemed more like a wide shelf because it had no rail. The dirt floor below looked hard and far away, and suddenly Mouse said, "This would be a perfect hideout."

Rolf looked at her. "You're right."

"We'd have to camouflage the steps." She was turning slowly around, looking at everything. "And clean it up. It'd be fun."

Tim sat down on the edge of the shelf and Rolf and Mouse sat down beside him. Tim picked up some crumbly stone fragments and sent them flying down. "Try and hit that middle place where the ruts are," he said.

They tried for a time, but no one could get a stone in the rut. Rolf moved restlessly and stood up. They went back down and outside into bright sunshine, and Mouse looked at the building again.

"It looks like one of those historical places people pay to go in."

"Yeah," Rolf said, "I saw some in Mexico once. Temple ruins. People down there used to worship the sun. They built their temples up on hills just like this, to get as close to the sun as they could."

"Solar energy," Tim said. "If we built a plant on this hill, we'd make a fortune."

Rolf laughed, but Mouse was still thinking. "Maybe this isn't a sugar mill — maybe it's a temple ruin. How far is Mexico from here?"

"A long way," Rolf said. "Down through the Leeward Islands, all the way across the Gulf of Mexico, to Yucatán." Then he added casually, "That's where I'm going. I only stopped here to fix the main winch on my boat."

There was a startled silence. Then Tim asked, "Are you going to sail there, or what?"

"Sail," Rolf answered. "I've already left home," he added.

"Oh," Tim said.

Mouse sat down in the grass, filled with sudden delight. So there *was* something special about him. She was so pleased she turned around to smile at him, but he was looking west across the bay, which was shining now in the afternoon sun. The breeze blew past them, and a curlew called farther along the hill.

Tim broke the silence. "Well, how will you do it? I mean eating, and living, and . . ." His voice trailed off. "Unless it's none of our business."

"That's okay," Rolf said. "I've got stores for the trip, but I try to save them. I've been living off the land. I pick stuff, and drink a lot of coconut milk."

Mouse remembered the Pepsis and peanut butter he had offered them last night. That must have been from his saved-up stores.

Rolf's voice broke in on her. "We'd better go back to the boat. I don't like to leave her too long in a place I don't know."

She got up and they jogged down the hill, but when they arrived at the beach the boat was just as it had been left, scarcely moving on her anchor line. Zec flew with loud cries to Rolf's shoulder, and the boy bent for a mangrove root.

"Here you go," he said, using his knife to get out the oyster.

"He looks as though he's trying to talk," Mouse said.

"I know. But he doesn't seem to learn." Rolf threw the gull into the air. He flew in a graceful circle around their heads, while they stood on the sand and watched him. Then he landed on the *Windsong*'s mast. They swam out after him, and hauled up the sails. The wind was from the northwest, but it was dying with the afternoon. Tim and Mouse had learned all they wanted for one day, and now they sat near Rolf in the cockpit, watching the cloud shadows make weird patterns on the main island.

They could see the endless chain of coves and bays with their crescent beaches, and the different shades of blue as the water changed depth. Sometimes, as they watched the main island come closer, they saw bright spots of red or yellow against the mountains — roofs of houses, reflecting the late light.

Mouse felt suddenly sleepy and eased onto the deck and lay with her face on her arms. She let one leg hang over the side, and hitched into her shirt. The air was cooler now. Sometimes the boat heeled and the water washed over, but the gunwale kept Mouse dry. She rolled over to watch the sun as it dropped toward the long western arm of the bay, and she decided that this island was the most beautiful place she had ever seen. It made her feel like melting into its blue-green world and staying here, forever.

She could hear the boys talking in the cockpit, their voices sounding like the waves that hit the boat and fell away again. Once a fish jumped to the surface, dripping purple colours, quickly swallowed by the sea. Rolf saw it too, for she heard him shout, "Ho, fish, thar — gone over!" She wondered what that expression meant.

Then she dozed. When she woke up the sun had pulled the clouds down, and the water had turned dark, jelled by the day's heat. The sky was soft now over the mountains, a pale clear color with the brilliance gone.

The breeze took them halfway into the beach by the cliff and now the air from the land came, bringing a warm green smell across the water. Mouse could hear a donkey hee-hawing somewhere, and it was the only sound she heard until Tim let down the anchor line.

Mouse licked her lips, tasting the salt, and walked to the stern. "I wish it wasn't over," she said.

"It isn't." Rolf was holding the main sheet, working the sail back and forth. "It's always like this."

Tim came back too. "Okay, we'll meet day after tomorrow, then." Mouse realized they must have made plans while she was asleep.

Rolf nodded. "Be here early. We'll need time to beat up the coast."

"Okay."

Tim and Mouse swam ashore, and turned to wave. Then Tim started for the cliff.

"Come on, we're late as the dickens."

"I know," Mouse said, still watching Rolf working on the deck, "but I wish we didn't have to go at all."

Six

At the hotel, a message was waiting. Dad and Mom were delayed again at the office and wouldn't be back for dinner.

"Your parents want you to eat without them," the desk clerk said. "And don't wait up."

"We're lucky," Tim said in the dining room. "I'm not sure what we would have said about getting back so late."

"I thought we were going to tell Dad, especially if we're going again," Mouse said.

"Right." Tim looked serious. "But what're we going to say? We sent this boy a message and he took us sailing? You told us not to but we went anyway?"

"Mmn," Mouse said, imagining Dad's face.

"I think we should learn to sail first, since Rolf said he'd teach us," Tim went on. "Then when we're really good we'll take Dad out and surprise him."

Mouse pushed her chair back. "Dad'll see through that in a minute."

"Maybe so, but you know Dad would think Rolf's too young to teach us. And there's another thing. I'm not sure Rolf wants anyone to know about him, even Dad. Maybe especially a person like Dad."

Tim was right, Mouse thought. Wherever Rolf had come from, wherever he was going, it was his own business. They had no right to do anything that would ruin his plans. She sighed. She had a sinking feeling that they were already in too deep.

But maybe not. Maybe there was still a way out. She looked at Tim. "Why don't we talk to Rolf about it? Maybe he wouldn't mind meeting Dad, and showing Dad how well he can sail. Did he say what he's doing tomorrow?"

"He said he was going to town. He has some things to get."

"We should go to town too, then." Mouse ate a last dessert cookie and got up. "If we can find him, we'll ask him how he feels about meeting Dad."

"Okay," Tim said. "But if he doesn't want to, that's it. We're not saying anything to Dad about our sailing."

She nodded, and they left the dining room to putter restlessly through a game of Ping-

Pong and some television. They postponed any questions about their day by being asleep when their parents came home, but the next morning Mr. Randolph looked serious when Tim and Mouse came downstairs.

"Mom and I want to talk to you," Dad said.

Mouse's heart did a flip-flop in her chest.

Dad led the way onto the terrace, and they followed, their thoughts racing. Had someone seen them yesterday? How could Dad have found out so fast?

But then Tim realized that Dad was talking about the office, explaining that matters had come to a head with the island's businessmen.

"The meeting last night confirmed what we've been suspecting," Dad was saying. "Our company's plans are at a standstill here, at least until after the election."

Mouse's heart stopped thumping quite so hard.

"So Mom and I have decided to do some cost rundowns with other Caribbean governments, to see what else is available. That means taking survey trips to six or seven other islands."

Tim's voice was tense. "When?" he said.

"As soon as possible," Mom answered. "We're waiting on plane reservations, hopefully for tomorrow."

"But we can't!" Mouse said desperately. "I mean, I thought we were going to be here all summer."

"Dad, listen." Tim clutched his father's arm. "Couldn't we stay? We know the hotel by now, and we'd be fine. You could do business better without us anyway, and we wouldn't mind being here alone. It'd be fun."

Dad looked startled, and then he started to laugh. "As a matter of fact, that was one of the possibilities we talked about, and we were wondering how you'd feel about it. Our trip's going to be rushed, and we couldn't really sight-see, or do much with you."

"Only we'd want you to stay with Captain Fisher, instead of at the hotel," Mom said. "He has a housekeeper, and it wouldn't be too much trouble."

Mouse felt weak with relief. "Has he said it's okay?"

Mom nodded. "We'll call him to confirm it. Then you ought to pack this afternoon."

Tim's face broke into a wide grin. "That is *so* great."

Dad smiled back at him. "Margaret, what are we going to do with our children?"

"Give us jewels and a bucket of popsicles," Mouse said. "And a new dog."

"Of course," Mom laughed. "Such modest wants."

Mouse kissed her. "I love you," she said.

"Me too," Mom said lightly, but her hug was warm.

When Mom and Dad had left, Tim and Mouse stood and looked at each other.

"Saved," Tim said. "Now we can sail all we want. Let's go to town anyway, and find Rolf."

"I hope Captain Fisher's not going to be nervous about us," Mouse said.

"He's used to it here. I don't think he'll care as much what we do," Tim said.

They got out their bicycles and pedalled rapidly toward town, along the dusty coast road. It had been paved once, but the sand had spread over it again and now it was white, between rows of green trees. The road followed the land, sloping uphill first, and then down into the town. Tim and Mouse coasted into the first narrow streets, but shortly they had to slow down. Goats, donkeys, babies, people walked in and out of open doorways, or seemed to be making their home in the middle of the street. Everywhere people were talking, smiling or laughing, and some of them were shouting. Mouse liked the noise and confusion, and she grinned back at a boy who said hello to her.

She and Tim got off and walked, pushing their bikes until they reached the center of town, a large, wide square near the water-front. First they circled it, looking up the side streets for Rolf. Then they looked in different shops. Tim found a hardware shop and a ship's supply store, and Mouse looked in the grocery store, the pharmacy, and even the post office. But Rolf was nowhere around, and after a half hour they met, hot and thirsty, at the square. Tim bought some Cokes, and they sat on a stone bridge over a gutter that poured into the sea.

Mouse took off her sandals and spread her toes along the stone. She put her head on her knees, hugging her legs with her arms. A large paper cup was floating along upside down under the bridge, and its shape reminded her of the old sugar mill.

"If we're going to sail with Rolf," she said, "why couldn't we use that old tower as a place to go? Remember how he said it reminded him of Mexico?"

Tim nodded.

"Well, we could really fix it up, sort of decorate it. Then maybe Rolf would like it and stay around longer."

Tim looked blank. "But what would we decorate it with?"

"Maybe we could get a book about Mexico and see what it's like there. You know, the places and stuff."

Tim looked thoughtful. "That's not a bad idea. Did you bring any money?"

She shook her head. "If there's a library, we could look there."

Tim got up. "I'll ask."

He found a policeman in a sun helmet, who directed them to a back street, and a small two-storey building. They went up some steps to a big room with lots of windows and a cool breeze. Outside Mouse could see the sea, sparkling blue in the distance. The librarian produced two books on Mexico, a big heavy one and a small thin one, and they sat down at a shining black table that smelled of turpentine.

Tim opened the big one. The print was very small and it was written by a Professor Bartlett, the heading said, in 1922. The sentences were long and mostly about the excitement he had felt on entering the jungles of the Pacific coast.

"It would take a year to read this," Tim said.

"We want pictures, anyway," Mouse said. "Try the other one."

The second book was better. On the first page was a map, and in the back were colour photographs of huge pyramids.

"Those must be those ruins Rolf talked about," Tim said. "Wow, look at those names." He was turning the pages, looking at pictures of huge altars and statues. "Tequcigalpa and Xicalanco. Huitzlopochtli. I wonder if he's ever heard of that."

"Let's find out how to take this book out," Mouse said.

It turned out to be easy. The librarian typed their name and addresses on a card, and said they could bring the book back in two weeks.

"That's lots of time," Mouse gloated as they clattered down the steps. "I just hope Rolf likes it."

They took a last swing around the square and then pedalled back to the hotel to pack. By midafternoon Mom had settled everything, and they were on their way to Captain Fisher's house.

"I'm not going to tell you what you should and shouldn't do," Dad was saying from the front seat of the car. "Captain Fisher knows this island better than we do. I rented the bikes for a month so you could get around on your own, but remember Captain Fisher's completely in charge. What he says, goes."

"Right," Tim said.

Captain Fisher had asked them all for supper, and afterward Mom and Dad stayed for a while to talk. Then they got up to go.

"Behave," Dad said to Tim and Mouse.

"And have fun," Mom added. "We'll see you in two or three weeks."

Mouse felt a lump in her throat. For a minute she felt like a little girl who wanted desperately to go everywhere her mother went. Then she remembered Rolf, and instead she gave Mom a tight hug.

"Have a good time," she said.

Then Mom and Dad were gone, and Tim and Mouse stood with Captain Fisher on the verandah, waving until the car vanished into the tropical night. For a minute there was a silence. Captain Fisher turned around.

"Going away reminds me of that boy I delivered the message to," he said suddenly. "Did you ever meet up with him?"

Tim froze.

"Is something wrong?" Mouse said.

"Yes. He's run away from home. There's an All Points Bulletin out on him — came in this afternoon. It's that same boy, no question about it. The boat description is perfect."

"Wow," Mouse said, trying to act surprised. "Run away!"

Tim thought fast. "We did see him after that. He was sailing around the bay. Where do you think he is now?"

"Probably the cove where I found him that day. Looked like he was using it for an anchorage. Anyway" — Captain Fisher led the way into the house — "the Coast Patrol's asked me to search this area because I'm the only person around here with big boats. They're concentrating west of the bay, and to the south."

He was in the hall by now and he turned to face Tim and Mouse. "So, that cove's where I'm going to start looking, first thing in the morning."

Rolf walked along the edge of the beach, looking for conches in the shallow water. It was late afternoon, and he had been hunting the big pink shellfish for some time, hoping to find enough for a meal. This year conches were scarce everywhere, he had noticed. He hoped they weren't getting fished out.

Zec followed, sometimes flying in circles around the boy's head, sometimes riding on his shoulder. Soon he grew tired of this pilgrimage, or bored, and flew along the water's edge, looking for fish. Rolf saw him dive and come up with a silver slab, and the boy laughed.

"If I don't feed you, you'll find it yourself, is that it? That's more than most pets will do when their owners are running out of food."

Early that morning Rolf had gone to a tiny village in the opposite direction from town to buy the winch part he needed in a little boatyard there. Unnoticed, he had left quickly, and by noon he was back at the boat, setting to work on the broken gear. When he had repaired it, he was very hungry, and he had started out again to look for food.

Now his toes hit something in the water, and he bent to dig up a half-buried shell. It was a big conch, but it was empty. Tired, he sat down, and held the glistening pink spiral to his ear. He loved to hear the roaring, and imagine he was sailing the *Windsong* beyond the reefs, in the wildest of storms. It would be terrifying, he knew, but somehow it always seemed wonderful to think about.

Zec flew to the beach, interrupting Rolf's thoughts. He came to the boy's feet, and began walking slowly on the sand. Finally he perched on Rolf's foot, and he too looked out to sea, turning his head this way and that.

The sunset breeze ruffled Rolf's hair, and

he ran his hand over his head. This was almost his favourite time, in the late afternoon. Two years ago he and his father had sailed all around these islands, and sunset had been one of the best times of day. That was the time when they were picking an anchorage, and starting to think about what they were going to have for supper.

But now it was different. Now he was alone. Except for Zec, and Tim and Mouse. They were nice— he liked them. It was too bad he hadn't met them sooner. If he weren't leaving, he would like to do more with them. But there was no way he could stay much longer. If he waited to head south, the hurricane season would start, and he might never get to Mexico at all.

Rolf sat for so long he saw the sun go down and the pale moon begin to shine in the luminous afterglow. Then he stood up to stretch. It was a long way to his boat, and he began to walk rapidly, with Zec on his shoulder.

It was dark when he got to the *Windsong*. The emptiness of the beach made him feel suddenly lonely, and he spoke just to hear his own voice. "It looks all by itself, the way we are, Zec."

He swam slowly out to the *Windsong* on his

back, holding one arm out of the water for Zec's perch. His stroking legs made phosphorous trails in the moonlit water, and the flickering lights were so interesting to watch that he came to the boat before he knew, and bumped his head against the hull.

"Ouch!" He laughed and threw the sea gull to the deck. "Up you go, Zec. We didn't do too well about food, did we? We'll have to see what we can find here."

He went down to the galley and lit the lantern that hung over the primus stove. The light flickered on the tiny sink and the big copper pan where the ice went, when he had any. It was empty, since he hadn't gone to town to buy ice.

He reached into the cupboard under the primus, and brought out a hard slab of chocolate and two bananas. From a bin he got a coconut, and took the food up on deck to the bow.

He poked three tiny holes in the coconut with his knife and drained the milk into a mug. Then he lifted a long machete above his shoulder and aimed carefully. Holding his tongue between his teeth in concentration, with a sudden movement he brought the machete sharply down, slicing through the nut as cleanly as any saw. The meat inside showed white in the moonlight, and Rolf sat down to eat.

When he had finished, he leaned his back against the mast. Off on the hills the moon showed the tops of the trees like miniature feather dusters, and the boy wondered what was happening in the houses that lay beneath. The cove was silent around him in the moonlight, and the beach looked silvery across the clear stretch of water. He lay back with his head on a coil of rope, looking up at the stars. Which was Orion? he wondered. Maybe he ought to go below and get that book in the trunk, the one about the stars. But he felt tired, and lay trying to find them by himself. Finally he found the Southern Cross, and he fell asleep.

He was awakened by a noise. He opened his eyes, and saw the first faint grey of dawn. Seabirds called across the water, but that was not what had wakened him. Then he heard it again. A voice, coming from the beach. "Hey, Rolf!"

He struggled up and looked over the cockpit. He saw a figure standing on the sand. It was Tim, waving.

"Hi!" Rolf called. "Be right there."

He slid across to the rail and dived into the water, and swam ashore. Tim was shivering from early morning chill, but his voice was clear.

"They're after you," he said.

"Who is?"

"Captain Fisher. Or at least somebody. I guess it's your family. There's an All Points Bulletin out, and Captain Fisher's coming over here as soon as it's day. So I came early to tell you."

"That was really nice of you," Rolf said. "Thanks."

"Mouse stayed at Captain Fisher's, in case anyone looks in our room," Tim went on. "But she thinks you ought to go to the sugar mill. I do, too."

Rolf was silent. He looked down the coast, as though he were thinking. He walked two or three steps along the beach. Then he turned around.

"That's a good idea, but I think I should head south. That's where I'm going anyway."

"You can't," Tim said. "At least not right now. Coast Patrol boats are looking down there."

"Are they all after me?" Rolf looked worried.

"We don't know yet, but I know they're going to look along the beaches. That's why we thought of the little island."

"Okay." Rolf nodded. "It's a good idea. But there's one thing . . ."

"What?"

"I don't have much food. I've got money on the boat, but if you could get me some stuff, I'll sail back here tonight when it's dark and pay you."

"Sure," Tim said. "Don't worry about the money. Dad left us some. What do you need?"

Rolf told him bread and powdered milk, and some canned things. And ice. "If you could get some butter too, I'd really love that."

"We will," Tim said. He hitched up his shorts, and looked around. "Listen, it's getting a lot lighter, you better go. We'll get everything and meet you here tonight."

Seven

When Tim turned his bike into Captain Fisher's driveway, he could see Mouse sitting on the porch steps, nervously chewing her hair. She jumped up when she saw him, and ran toward him.

"Captain Fisher's inside," she said. "I said you were still asleep. What happened?"

Tim got off his bike, sweat dripping down his face from the long ride. "Rolf went to the little island, and he wants us to get him some stuff. I better get out of sight — "

Captain Fisher strode onto the porch, carrying an orange wet suit and some compression tanks. He put them down with a thump, and squinted up at the drive at Tim.

"Morning," he called. "Glad you're up and about. I'm taking off. What're you two going to do today?" He stopped and looked at them, rubbing his chin. "I mean, what *do* you usually do all day?"

It suddenly occurred to Tim that Captain

Fisher had no idea what to do with children. "We'll be all right by ourselves," he was starting to say, when a better idea popped into his head. ". . . And we were really hoping to find a rowboat," he finished.

"A rowboat," Captain Fisher said. He sounded relieved. "That's right, I remember now, you said you'd like to have a little runabout. Well, that's an easy problem to remedy. There are a couple of little skiffs down at the wharf, and nobody's using them. I'll send you out with one of my men so you can learn how to run one and where to go" — he was carrying his compression tanks to the car, talking all the while — "not for deep water, you understand, but at least you won't be dependent on me for your amusement."

"Right," Tim said. "That's what we were thinking too."

Captain Fisher put the wet suit in the back of the car and closed the trunk. "Good. Get whatever you want for the day, and I'll take you down in the car with me."

"A boat!" Mouse followed Tim into the house. "I can't believe it!"

"I'm a genius," Tim said. "Everyone knows it but you. Hurry up, get our sunburn stuff while I get some money for Rolf's food. We'll get it after we're in town."

When they arrived at the Salvage Company docks, Captain Fisher introduced them to a short, pleasant-looking man named John Wade, who shook hands with Tim and Mouse and picked up a set of oars. He motioned them into a skiff that was tied up below the wharf, but Tim stopped short, not believing his eyes. It had an outboard motor! "Is that our boat?" he said.

"Right," Captain Fisher boomed. "Hop in, and keep busy. I have a lot to do."

"Well," Tim said, so pleased he couldn't think of anything else to say. "Thanks a lot."

"That's all right," Captain Fisher said. "See you tonight."

He waved, and they waved back. Mouse felt suddenly worried. Suppose Rolf wasn't hidden well enough? But Mr. Wade was standing right beside them, so she couldn't say anything to Tim.

They got in the skiff and Mr. Wade showed them how to start the engine — by giving a hard jerk on the starter cord — and how to work the throttle. It was a bar with a rubber grip that turned ahead for forward and backward for reverse.

"This skiff is flat bottomed, so you can't hit much," Mr. Wade said amiably. "I'll let you take her out."

Tim took the throttle bar and put the skiff out from the dock. It was small, and not as strong as the *Windsong*, but it felt steady and the little engine seemed smooth. Mr. Wade lit a pipe while they put-putted past the town, heading along the shoreline of the bay. He pointed out how the bottom gradually dropped off from shore, at first pale and clear, then deepening into dark patches of sea grass. Deeper still, the water was a dark blue-green colour, and the bottom was too far below to see.

"Stay over the sea grass, or even closer to shore," Mr. Wade suggested. "Skiffs are built for shallow water. Not much draft, so they don't handle well where there's swells or current. No need to go so far out anyway — nothing to go out there for. Keep close in, and you'll be fine."

Tim brought the boat nearer to land, and Mr. Wade began to ask them all about themselves and their lives in Chicago. While Tim was answering, Mouse noticed that the boatman was looking in every cove, every inlet and along every beach that they passed. Casually Mouse glanced out toward the small green islands by the reef. Nothing showed where Rolf was. There was not a sign of a blue hull or a white sail, just sky and water shimmering in the sun.

She looked back at Mr. Wade. Now he was talking to Tim about American sports. They discussed soccer, and then football, Tim's favourite.

"You must be good," Mr. Wade commented.

Tim shook his head with a rueful grin. "Not very. I'm too skinny. No weight."

Mr. Wade glanced at him. "You look all right to me."

"Thanks, but I'm not. I'd rather be doing stuff like this, anyway." Tim waved his hand at the bay and the boat.

Mr. Wade smiled. "It's a good life. I wouldn't live anywhere else. Neither would they." He pointed to two big sea turtles swimming side by side in the green water. He explained they were headed for the reef, to feed on a special kind of seaweed that grew nearby.

Then he began to talk about the big turtles — where they lived, no one knew, and how far they could swim. Tim listened, liking the feel of the sun on his head and the throttle in his hand. Mr. Wade seemed satisfied with the way he was handling the boat, only suggesting that he keep going toward the far western end of the bay. After an hour, they reached the outer point. Tim rounded it, hugging the shore, and Mr. Wade pulled a pair of binoculars out of his pocket. He sat up very straight, studying the coastline to the south. Tim and Mouse exchanged glances. He was looking for Rolf. It couldn't be anything else. They sat quietly, pretending not to know. Mouse was surprised to see how close the reef was out here. An idea started coming into her mind when Mr. Wade put his glasses away and suggested they start back. Tim throttled up and turned the skiff around.

"You're doing well," Mr. Wade said.

It was after noon when they got back to Captain Fisher's wharfs, but Mr. Wade decided on a final boating test. He made Tim and Mouse check their life jackets, and then he ordered them to jump overboard in what he called a "lifeboat drill." After they scrambled, dripping, back into the skiff, he seemed satisfied.

"Take the boat out on your own for a bit," he said. "I'll keep an eye on you."

"Thanks, but we've got an errand in town," Tim said. "Is tomorrow okay?"

"Fine. The Captain said to use it all you like."

They walked into town to buy Rolf's supplies, and then started the long trek back to Captain Fisher's house.

"I wish that skiff could go uphill," Mouse panted. "But at least we can really get around on the water now."

"I'm worried," Tim said. "Rolf's island's across the deepest part of the bay. And Mr. Wade's going to see us if we try it."

"But we don't have to go that way," Mouse said. "Remember this morning how close we were to the reef? Well, we can do the same thing in the other direction. We can go past the hotel and the cliff, to the other point. The reef's probably really close out there too. We can cross over and follow it back to Rolf's island. It'll be safe — we could always land on the reef if anything happens."

Tim was silent, thinking. "Okay," he said. "That's a good idea. Nobody'll see us way over there, either."

By the time they got back to Captain Fisher's house it was too late to go swimming, so they hung around the garden, listening to the town noises drifting up the hill and waiting for Captain Fisher to come home. Finally his car turned into the driveway, and Captain Fisher drew up in front of the house.

"We didn't find the boy," he announced.

"There wasn't a sign of him anywhere."

"Maybe he's gone home," Tim said.

"Do you know where the All Points Bulletin came from?" Mouse asked.

"The bulletins come out of Kingston," Captain Fisher said, climbing out of his car. "But that doesn't mean a thing. They just come across the police Teletype. Maybe a detailed report will come through in a day or two. But anyway" — he headed up the steps — "wherever he's from, it's my opinion that he's not around here anymore."

Before supper Tim went into the storeroom behind Captain Fisher's kitchen, and looked until he found an ice chest. He waited until after supper to fill it with ice cubes and strap it on his bike rack. When it was dark, Mouse put the food bag and the library book in her bike basket, and they slipped away, pedalling through the hot tropical night.

Below the cliff Rolf was waiting for them. The *Windsong* was pulled close in to shore, and Tim and Mouse waded out to stow everything in the cabin.

"Captain Fisher thinks you've left," Mouse said.

"And we've got a skiff," Tim said. "We're going to try to come over tomorrow."

Rolf looked pleased.

Mouse handed him the library book. "It's about Mexico," she said. "We thought you might like it."

"Thanks." Rolf put it on the seat. Then he looked up at the cliff. "I'd better not stay here long. You never know who's watching."

"Right," Tim said. He and Mouse helped push the *Windsong* off, and Rolf jumped on the stern.

"Make sure nobody follows you tomorrow," he called.

"Don't worry," Tim called back. He grinned at Mouse, standing in the water. "Boy, if we get caught now, Dad would be so mad he'd never get over it. And Captain Fisher'd probably throw us all in jail."

"Or eat us." Mouse shivered happily.

Tim stood up in the back of the skiff, studying the water running ahead by the point. His hand was on the throttle bar, and his eyes were feasting on the sight of the morning sky and the ocean, and the reef not fifty yards away.

He took a deep breath. They had done it. He could hardly believe where they were. Just as Mouse had predicted, they had found they could take the skiff around the bay to the outer point, and now they had only a little stretch of deep water to cross before they reached the reef. Coral rocks were jutting up all around them, but Tim didn't feel nervous. Having the skiff was great, and somehow it made him feel as though he could do everything better than he ever had before. He throttled forward, and felt a swell of current start to catch them as they left the shelter of the point. He picked up more speed, legs braced against the seat, holding the bar with both hands. The skiff slid sideways for a minute, but then she steadied, and Tim swung her back into her course.

Mouse sat crouched in the bow, eyes glued to the surface ahead. "Go left a little," she called, then, "Go right. Hold it straight. Wait a min — " She let out her breath. They had passed over a huge boulder, looming like a giant mossy monster under their gunwales. Now the water was so deep it was dark blue. Mouse wondered how far down the bottom was. She tried not to think about it, or to wonder if anyone could see them from town. She chanced a quick look across the bay, and decided they were too far away to be seen clearly.

She felt the skiff shudder from a fresh current, and her eyes jumped back to the water ahead. It was becoming pale green. Mouse saw a school of fish darting in circles. The current slacked off. She looked up, and saw that they had reached the reef.

The white coral line rose out of the water, in places as high as two feet. On the ocean side the surf was bouncing up in high plumes of spray, but inside it was calm, and the water was clear. Fish were everywhere, swimming alongside the reef or moving in and out of its cavernous holes.

Tim kept the skiff at high speed, and in minutes they came to the channel between the reef and the little islands. Now no one could see them from the bay, and he slowed down. He found the little cove and turned in, heading confidently for the beach. Rolf had moored the *Windsong* off to one side of the cove behind three big black coral rocks, where she was barely moving on the anchor line. Zec moved sideways along the main boom, making his mewing noises, but Rolf was nowhere in sight.

"He can't be far away," Tim said. "Let's try the sugar mill."

He put the skiff right up to shore and Mouse

jumped out, pulling the bow on the sand. She made the line fast on a mangrove branch, and they headed into the palm trees and up the hill. Suddenly they almost ran into Rolf, bent over a puddle. He jumped up.

"Hi. I thought this might be a freshwater spring, but it's not."

"We could have brought water in bottles," Tim said.

Rolf shook his head. "We need too much. For washing, and for getting salt off everything."

Tim wondered how a boy who had run away and sailed his own boat across the Caribbean could worry so about washing. It must be the boat—sailors were notoriously neat, always swabbing decks.

"Yes," Mouse was saying, "and for brushing our teeth."

"Brushing our teeth!" Tim said. "I'm not brushing any teeth over here."

Rolf smiled. "You don't have to," he said. He studied the trees. "There ought to be water somewhere. If we spread out, we can probably find it."

They went farther into the trees and separated, quartering up over the hill and down the other side. They looked in high grass, under rocks and in bushes, and even poked sticks in the ground. Mouse surprised a crane-like bird with two gawky chicks on their nest, and Tim saw a colony of grotesque-looking land crabs. Rolf spotted some pineapple plants and cut off two large, juicy pineapples. But they didn't find water.

"Couldn't we dig for it?" Tim asked, when they met in front of the sugar mill.

"On these little islands the water would come up salty," Rolf answered. "It's not like the main island, with mountains and rivers."

He was slicing one of the pineapples in three parts, and they buried their faces in the sweet yellow fruit. He sliced another, and they sat down in the grass to eat it.

Rolf looked up at the stone tower. "I came up here this morning to read that book you brought. It's good."

"Is it like this place?" Mouse asked.

"Quite a bit," he said. "Those ruins in Mexico were places for ceremonies and stuff, but it looks the same." He went in the mill and came out with the book, flipping the pages.

"Here." He stopped at one of the drawings. It showed three figures standing in front of a statue of a huge bird, with a stone tower behind.

"All we need is the statue," Mouse said. "Maybe we could make one, out of rocks."

Rolf looked puzzled. "We could, but why do you want it to be like Mexico here?"

Mouse stared at him, feeling suddenly confused. "Well, we thought you'd . . . I mean, we thought it would remind you of where you want to be."

"Oh," Rolf said. He looked at Tim, who had taken the book and was sprawled in the grass reading.

"*Hu-it-zil-opo-chtle*," he pronounced slowly, "The cult of human sacrifice."

Mouse's back tingled and she couldn't help looking around the grassy hill. "Maybe not that part," she said. "But if we brought canned food, and put some mats around to sit on, it could be our own private place away from everything. We could use it for messages . . ."

"Messages for who?" Tim said.

"I don't know, each other—if one of us found out something."

Tim got up. There were yellow flowers sticking out of his hair, and green stains on his shorts. Rolf grabbed Mouse's arm.

"Shh," he said. "Someone's here."

A black girl stood just below the hilltop, staring at them.

"Who are you?" Rolf leaped to his feet. "How did you get here?" His tone was threatening, but she just stood and looked at them.

"I'm Parry," she said finally. "I stay here."

"On this island?" Tim asked.

"Alone?" Rolf said.

"No, with my granpa, and my brother. What are you here for?"

"We just came," Rolf said.

There was a silence.

"Well, look, we just wanted to know how you saw us," Tim said.

"We saw your boat," Parry said. "We've been waiting for you to leave. But you didn't, and we needed water, so I came up here."

"Water!" Rolf nearly shouted. "Where is it? Will you show us?"

"All right." She led the way behind the sugar mill, past the spot where Tim had found the land crabs, and halfway down the slope on the other side. There, under a clump of low thorn bushes that straggled over the hillside, she pointed to a hidden spring. It bubbled up and back into a little pool that seemed to drain underground.

"Wow," Tim said.

"We never would have found that," Rolf said.

"But Parry did," Tim said. He smiled at the girl, who smiled back.

The boys bent down to taste the water, and Mouse cupped her hands and drank too. "It's good." She turned to Parry. "All we've had is Pepsis and coconut milk."

Parry dipped in her bucket. "Granpa says too much coconut milk is bad for you. I like it a lot."

Rolf was rubbing wet dirt from his knees. "Where is your Granpa?"

Surprisingly, Parry started walking away. They followed, suspicious again.

"Hey, where're you going?" Tim said.

She halted, her eyes blazing furiously. "You're not going to find him. He does not wish publicity." And then, almost sullenly, "Good-bye."

Tim and Mouse stared at her, but Rolf smiled. "We're hiding too, you know. We won't tell. Please come back."

At his words she turned around and faced them again. She began to tug on her short cotton dress.

"I want to take the water back," she said. "But you can come with me if you like." She picked up her bucket and started down the hill. Rolf gestured to Tim and Mouse to follow, and he fell into step beside her.

"How old are you?" he said.

"Twelve."

He nodded. "I'm thirteen, and Tim's twelve."

Parry looked at Mouse, who held up two fingers. "Eleven."

"Brother is eight," Parry finished solemnly. "I don't know about Granpa."

At the bottom of the hill, she led them through a large, shallow inlet. Palm fronds rustled gently in the breeze, and the sunlight dappled the shallow water, where myriads of shells lay on the clear bottom. Mouse picked up a pale pink Double Sunrise shell, and then put it back. It was too fragile to carry around all day.

In a few minutes more, they reached a small thatched house. It sat in the trees, looking across a wide stretch of sand to the reef and the ocean beyond. A dinghy was pulled up on the beach, and a small boy was sitting on the doorstep, wearing bright flowered shorts.

"This is Brother," Parry said.

A tall black man came through the open door. He was wearing a bathing suit, and smiling.

"And Granpa," Parry said formally.

They told him their names, and Granpa motioned to a bench and some chairs.

"This is a beautiful spot," he was saying

conversationally. "Most tourists never see it."

Tim felt suddenly wary. Granpa seemed nice, but he might be trying to find out why they were there.

"It looks like a really good place for shells," Tim said.

"It is," Brother said.

Rolf had remained standing. "Does this island belong to anyone?"

The older man shook his head. "It is public land. Anyone can come here."

Granpa's measured voice puzzled Mouse. He talked like a schoolteacher, or someone who gave speeches on television. Except there wasn't any television here, so who was he? She shook her head and realized everyone was looking at her.

"Parry was asking if you would like to see our shells," Granpa said.

"Oh, yes." Mouse jumped up, and followed the others to a low table beside the little house. Mouse and Tim had never seen such perfect shells. All of them had a shiny washed look, as though they had been lifted out of clear water and clean sand that very morning. There were familiar-looking ones, small conchs and clams, and some kinds that Mouse had never seen before, odd and beautifully striped or spotted.

"We have to dive for those," Parry said.

Granpa put his arm around Brother's shoulders. "We're growing strong lungs," he said.

"Do you want me to show you how we get shells?" Brother sounded so eager they all smiled.

"Sure," Rolf said.

The boy ran toward a pile of face masks and swim fins that were lying on the beach. He put on one of the masks, which was made of glass and rubber and fastened behind his head with a strap, and pulled some rubber fins on his feet. He walked quickly into the water and plunged under the surface. He came up twenty yards away, and went down again. This time he was under so long that Rolf unconsciously took a step toward the water. Granpa laid a hand on the boy's arm.

"I am watching," he said. "Brother can hold his breath for a long time."

It seemed that he could. Long seconds went by until the dark head popped up, much farther to the right than they had expected. Brother waved wildly and swam sidestroke to the beach. When he reached the shallows, he unfolded one hand from his chest and held up a beautiful cream-coloured shell with soft purplish spots on its pale surface.

"That's a Junonia!" Parry said. "They're rare."

Brother came up to Mouse. "For you," he said, handing the shell to her. Mouse took it, turning it over in her hands. It seemed almost unreal, as though someone had handed her a valuable jewel. "It's beautiful," she said. "Thank you very much."

Tim turned to Granpa. "Diving looks like a lot of fun."

Granpa smiled. "Would you like to try?"

Tim felt Rolf touch his arm, and turned around. "We have some work to do on the boat," Rolf said. "We just put in to clean it up."

Granpa nodded. "Come again, any time."

They thanked him and walked back up the hill.

"What do you think?" Tim said when they were out of earshot. "Are they okay?"

"I'm not sure." Rolf frowned. "But the first thing to do is check the rest of the island, and find out if there are any other people here. And if their dinghy is the only boat out here."

Tim looked around. The sun was heading into afternoon, and he realized Mr. Wade might be wondering where they were.

"The trouble is, Mouse and I ought to get the skiff back," he said.

"That's okay. I can do it alone," Rolf said.

Mouse had fallen behind, admiring her Junonia shell. She caught up. "What do you think Parry meant about not wanting publicity?"

"It sounds like Granpa's famous," Tim said. "Maybe he's writing a book or something."

"Or maybe he's a political leader. A terrorist," Mouse said. "Except he doesn't seem like one."

"How would you know? You've never met a terrorist," Tim said.

They had reached the cove, and Zec flew across the water to meet them. Rolf absent-mindedly caught the gull and began stroking him. "What's bothering me is they could have a radio. And if they do, they could have heard the bulletin about me."

"How will we find out?" Tim started untying the skiff's line. "We can't ask."

"No, but maybe I can find out some other way. Like go back and ask if they've heard a weather report or something."

Tim nodded. "Yeah. But be careful."

"I will. If there's any trouble I'll capture them first." Rolf smiled suddenly, a flash of a grin that excited Mouse. A picture came in her mind of Rolf hauling Granpa away, and she laughed aloud at the thought.

But Tim was still worried. "All I can say is" — he frowned as he climbed in the skiff — "just make sure it's not the other way around."

Eight

Rolf paused at the top of the hill, shading his eyes against the sun. He had watched Tim and Mouse's skiff rapidly becoming smaller as it headed for the main island, and then he watched three tiny specks far to the west. They were launches, cruising in a row, and Rolf followed their progress until they turned in toward the town. No other unusual boats were in the bay, and he turned his attention to where he was. He should have sailed around the other little islands first, he reflected, but he had never dreamed any people would be here.

He went past the mill and down to the other side of the island, following the water's edge. Ahead of him a single little bird, a rail, was zigzagging along the sand. Rolf flipped a tiny shell toward it, but the bird only darted sideways, never stopping its pecking at the water's edge. Farther out, the waves boomed beyond the reef and Rolf knew there would be a breeze, but this side of the little island was flat and still, dreaming through the afternoon. The mangrove trees got thicker, hanging down over the water, and Rolf moved out to walk along a sandbar. When that dropped off he came back ashore, pushing through the branches again. A bird called, hidden in the trees. Rolf heard his own feet lapping in and out of the inlets and the sucking noise when he pulled a big shell out of the sand. When he threw it back again, the splash seemed to carry far into the distance, and he realized that if he kept his ears tuned, very little could take him by surprise. Even so, it took longer than he expected to look stealthily in each thicket, through every screen of trees, and around every inlet. But he kept at it until he had covered all of the island except for the part by Granpa's beach. He deliberately left that until last, and it was nearly sunset when he cut inland through the trees behind the little house. He found a place in the bushes and sat down, his back against a tree.

He could hear Granpa and Brother talking, and he peered out to see them rowing the dinghy by the reef. Parry was laying out something on the beach, and soon they hailed her, coming in. Rolf watched them beach the boat and lift out three large, reddish-yellow fish. Parry and Brother threw water at each other, and Granpa's strong laugh rose above their squeals. They came ashore, still laughing, and moved in and out of the little house, calling back and forth. The sun dropped into huge pink and purple clouds, and Rolf yawned and stretched, feeling a warm, damp breeze floating in from the reef. After a while Granpa went off down the beach, and Rolf watched Parry put charcoal in a burner. By now the daylight was fading, and when the flames finally caught, they glowed bright against the darkening eastern sky. Brother was working at the water's edge, cleaning the fish, and soon he moved closer into the firelight to see better. They were talking, and Rolf strained his ears to listen. Absorbed, he jumped when he realized that someone was walking up on him from behind.

It was Granpa. Trapped, Rolf stood up.

"Hello," Granpa said. "It's a lovely evening."

"Yes," Rolf said. There was a silence.

"I was just getting some fruit," Grandpa said. "We are about to have our dinner. Will you eat with us?"

"No, that's all right," Rolf said.

"We have much more than we can eat alone," Granpa went on as though he hadn't heard. "We had good fishing this evening."

Rolf turned, and suddenly a ripple of air brought the wonderful buttery smell of cooking fish. "Well, if you're sure," he said.

Granpa put his hand on Rolf's shoulder and walked him along toward the light. "I'm sure. We'd be happy to have you."

Parry and Brother had put a low table out on the beach and set it with tin plates between flowers and leaves. There was fruit and bread in bowls, and in the middle lay the big platter of steaming fish. Next to that was a pitcher of juice and some tin cups. Oil torches stood at either end, flickering gently in the soft air.

They ate sitting on the sand, watching the moon rise over the reef. The dinner was better than any food Rolf had tasted for a long time, and he ate hungrily. Granpa talked more than anyone else, teasing Brother and making plans with Parry. He treated Rolf with a reserved dignity, mostly making sure he was getting enough to eat. Rolf cast surreptitious glances around, looking for anything that could tell him more about who they were and what they were doing here. But there was nothing visible except the little hut, with its simple furniture and piles of shells outside. A fishing net hung from a tree, and diving gear was piled under that. It was almost as though they were here on a weekend outing. Finally Rolf took a deep breath.

"Do you have a radio?"

Granpa looked at him. "Yes," he said. "Why? Do you need it?"

"I might," Rolf answered, "To check the weather."

"You're welcome to use it. We only have it for emergencies."

Parry grinned. "Granpa likes the sounds of the sea and the birds better."

"You're right," Granpa chuckled. "I can predict the weather from the ocean and the sky, and we don't need to know about men's doings, out here." He waved his arm around at the lagoon.

Rolf shifted in his seat. "The hurricane season is coming though. Sometimes they're early."

"That is worth keeping in mind." Granpa picked up a mango and split it. "But I don't think we have to worry tonight."

He was still eating, talking now about the ways of hurricanes. Brother interrupted to tell about a storm he had been in, and Parry jumped up once to shoo away a huge land crab that had sidled toward the table. Rolf began to feel drawn into their circle, eating and talking, laughing and joking. When the food was gone, Parry went and got a guitar and Granpa began to play, accompanied by the moonlight. The lovely calypso rhythms seemed to match the breeze and the waves drumming on the reef, and soon Parry and Brother began to sing. Rolf found himself lying back on the sand, beating out the time with his fingers, relaxing in spite of himself.

Much later, he got up to leave. He felt so sleepy he almost thought he couldn't walk back to the cove. "Thanks very much," he said. "That was really nice."

Granpa got up too. "It was pleasant to have you." He smiled. "Use the radio any time. We will be diving tomorrow too, if you want to come back."

"Thanks."

When Rolf reached the *Windsong*, Zec was sleeping peacefully on the boom, and the water was quiet in the moonlight. Suddenly the boy realized that for the first time in weeks, he hadn't thought about his father. The familiar pain had gone, if only for a few hours.

He went below and stretched out on his bunk to think, but his head only seemed to hold the songs that Granpa had played, and his thoughts wandered off to tomorrow and the idea of diving. He hadn't done any for a long time — it might be fun to do it again. Then he realized he hadn't found out anything, really, about Granpa. Tomorrow would be time enough to worry, he decided, yawning, and minutes later he fell into a deep, dreamless sleep.

"How are things going with Mr. Wade?" Captain Fisher asked the next morning. He shifted gears and the car pulled out of the driveway onto the road to town.

"Fine," Tim said. "He's a nice guy, and he knows a lot about boats."

"Mrs. Shaw give you enough to eat last night?" Captain Fisher swerved to avoid two chickens that rushed out of a grove of banana trees and across the road.

"It was really good," Mouse said, remembering the housekeeper's dinner. "She gave us so much we couldn't eat it all."

The Captain seemed satisfied, and settled back to barreling down the road. "I'm not home very much," he said. "Especially now with the election coming up, I'm afraid I'll be home even less. Hope you kids don't mind."

"We don't mind at all," Tim said. "We're having a great time. By the way, did you hear any more about that boy?"

"Not yet," Captain Fisher shook his head. "But we will, sooner or later."

He had reached the town and concentrated on maneuvering through the streets, so the conversation died until they came to the wharfs.

"Here we are." Captain Fisher drew up in front of the main building and hopped out. "Afraid I'll be out again tonight, but Mrs. Shaw'll be there, of course. Have a nice day." He rushed off into his office.

The skiff was waiting for them, and Mr. Wade was busy, so it was easy to give him a casual wave and cast off without any questions. Tim backed out and circled into their course. The trip along the coast seemed shorter this time, probably, Mouse thought, because they had done it before, or maybe it was because they were straining to get to the cove and hear what Rolf had found. She still felt uneasy when they crossed the channel, but that went quickly too, and they had no trouble making the reef.

When they turned into the cove, the *Windsong* was quietly at anchor. Mouse let out her breath, hardly aware that she had been holding it. She could see Rolf cleaning the deck. He waved, and squeezed his mop over the rail.

"Everything's okay," he called. "There's nobody else on the island, and Granpa has a radio but he doesn't use it."

"Good." Tim beached the skiff. "I thought he seemed okay."

"No you didn't," Mouse said, turning around. "You were more worried about them than anyone else."

Rolf leaned farther over the rail. "They want us to come and dive with them."

"Great." Tim hopped out and tied the skiff's line, and Rolf came ashore with a set of rubber fins and a mask. "We can take turns with these. I haven't used them in a while but they'll still work."

At the lagoon Parry and Brother were already in the water, floating face down on the surface. They swam ashore when Rolf and Mouse and Tim arrived, and dug more masks and flippers out of a pile in the hut.

"Have you ever been to a reef?" Granpa said.

Tim and Mouse shook their heads.

"All right, we'll practice here first." He shoved the dinghy into the water and Parry held it in the shallows while Tim and Mouse put on their masks.

"Put only your faces in first, and look around," Granpa said.

Mouse came up beaming. "I can see everything! What's that black flower growing on the rocks?"

"That's a sea urchin," Granpa said. "Don't touch it — the spikes stick in you and burn."

He gave them snorkeling tubes and showed them how to adjust the mouthpiece around their teeth. Mouse put her face down and breathed, half-expecting water to come in. But it didn't, and she began to float, putting out her hand to touch some waving sea plants that grew on the bottom. Her fingers came nowhere near them, and she realized that the mask made everything look magnified and closer than it really was.

Rolf dipped his mask in the water, washing it out so it wouldn't fog up. He pulled the glass over his eyes and waded in. Tim dived after Rolf, up and under in long, easy rolls, finding his speed nearly doubled by the flippers. With the mask, it was as though there was no water at all, only the shells on the bottom, clearly outlined, and striped fish lazing around them, paying no attention to the swimmers at all. Tim followed Rolf out to deeper water and back, then circled around the dinghy while Granpa rowed slowly out to the reef. Parry and Brother followed, and Mouse lazed along behind. From underwater she could see Tim and Rolf's flippered feet thrusting down from the surface ahead and the clouds of bubbles where Granpa's oars were moving up and down.

At the reef Granpa dropped anchor and beckoned everyone to hang onto the dinghy's side. Each person, he said, would swim with a partner — Tim with Parry, Rolf with Brother, and Granpa with Mouse. No one was to go outside the reef, and everyone was to keep within an easy range of the anchored dinghy.

"I'll just check things first," he said, taking off his shirt. He slid into the water, flipped over, and dived. They saw a trail of bubbles slowly come up where he had gone down. His dark body was following the base of the reef — checking the current, Parry said. Suddenly he thrust upward and popped to the surface, expelling air with a great whoosh.

"Everything's fine at twenty-five feet," he said. "Go."

Rolf lifted a big net out of the dinghy, the long wooden handle riding easily on the surface, and swam off to fish with Brother.

Parry took three or four big gulps of air and went under. Tim tried to copy her, but his flippers sent him over too far and water came in his mask. He surfaced, sputtering.

"It takes practice," Granpa said. "You'll learn."

They kicked off from the dinghy and glided close to the greyish-white barrier, and when Mouse put her face in she could hardly believe what she saw. Underwater the reef was glowing with bright colour, and it was swarming with life. Dozens of kinds of fish swam in and out of its caverns, so many that it was impossible for Mouse to keep her eyes on any one for long. Plants, sponges, grass, and spidery sea fans clung to the coral's sides, and all types of shell creatures scurried for cover or oozed along its sandy base. Mouse floated slowly, trying to absorb everything at once. She saw a starfish, the first one she had ever seen alive. Its colour was a perfect camouflage against the sand and she watched, enchanted, as all five points moved along like a hula dancer. A long knifelike fish came up beside her, sawing his way through the water and breathing air bubbles, and then two blow-fishes went by, swelling up and down like miniature footballs.

Suddenly she saw a big ray, a huge black pancake flapping slowly along the bottom, and she backwatered hurriedly.

"He won't hurt you." Granpa's voice was beside her when she surfaced. "He's trying to get away from you too."

They watched the ray swim out of sight, and then Brother popped to the surface on the other side of the dinghy. "I've got a cray-fish!" he shouted.

Its claws were waving wildly in the air and he was having difficulty hanging onto its mid-dle. Granpa swam over to help him, but be-fore he got there Brother let go. The crayfish, a lobsterlike creature, rushed frantically away through the water, and everybody laughed.

They separated again, exploring the reef, resting, and diving. Tim and Parry's stays underwater grew longer and longer, for Tim was finding it easier to hold his breath. Granpa noticed it too.

"Where did you get lungs like that, in a

city?" he asked once when Tim was hanging on the dinghy to rest.

"I jog a lot," Tim said. "Maybe it comes from that."

"You have a good build for diving, too," Granpa said. "Tall and slim."

Tim felt a rush of pleasure. He had never thought of being skinny as being good for diving, but now that Granpa pointed it out, he realized it could be true. He went down with Parry again, helping her bring up coral. A pile was growing in the bottom of the dinghy, and Mouse climbed in to sort it out.

"What're you going to do with it?" she asked Parry.

"I don't know," the black girl smiled. "I just like it."

"I could use some sponges, on my boat." Rolf had pushed back his mask and half-draped himself on the seat, out of breath. He looked at Mouse, his blond hair plastered to his head.

"I found a squid, if you want to see it."

"Where?"

"On the reef."

"You mean like an octopus?"

"It's only a baby. Come on."

They swam along the reef until he stopped

and pointed at a hole about two feet under the surface. Mouse squinted, trying to see more than just a shadowy mass. Rolf poked the net down, and suddenly she saw waving tentacles.

"Gross!" she said, backing up.

"They won't hurt you. They're good to eat."

He dug with the net for a while, but by now the squid was jammed back in its hole. Finally he gave up, and looked at Mouse.

"Do you like it here?" he said.

"Yes. It's the best place I've ever been."

"I think it's probably the best place in the world," he said.

Mouse floated. She wanted to ask him why he was leaving if he felt that way, only he looked as though he was going to say more himself. Then he turned around. Granpa was waving. "We'd better swim back," he said.

When they reached the dinghy, Granpa had hauled up the anchor. "I think we've had enough for one day," he announced.

No one really minded, because by now the land seemed the same as the water, and the water seemed the same as the sky. It all seemed together, something they could go in and out of all day long. They drifted in slowly, using their fins to glide and float, until they touched bottom and they were at the beach. They waded ashore, and carried everything up to the hut.

Rolf turned to Parry. "Do you want to come back to my boat with us?"

"Me too?" Brother sounded shy.

"Of course." Rolf grinned at him.

They crossed the sandbar under a blazing sun, and went up the hill to the spring. Parry and Mouse walked inside the mill.

"I like it here," Parry said. She saw the library book lying on the floor and picked it up.

"That's only a book about Mexico." Mouse started out again, not wanting another person to see it.

It was too late — Parry was flipping through the pictures, stopping to study the ones Mouse and Tim had noticed.

"You could make statues like that out of shells." She sounded thoughtful. "Mangrove mud would harden them nicely."

"It would?" Mouse looked at her. She hadn't thought about telling Parry that she wanted to decorate the mill, but now she had a feeling she might.

"Yes." Parry continued to survey the mill. "It only needs some really big shells for the top. I've got some, and we could get more."

"That's a great idea. I didn't know about the

mud. And I want to decorate the whole inside too."

They went back to the spring, making plans. The boys were having a pebble-throwing contest, until suddenly Brother said, "Race you" and took off down the hill. Rolf and Tim tore after him, running faster and faster until Brother lost his balance and fell forward, rolling, laughing, picking himself up, and running on. Mouse and Parry plunged down behind them and no one stopped until they reached the beach and crashed into the water, lying in a circle splashing at each other.

Finally they grew tired of it. "What started us?"

"We've gone crazy."

"I like being crazy."

Mouse turned over and put her head in the water, holding her breath. When she straightened up, her hair streamed down her face and neck, and she pushed it back, wiping her face with her hands. "I feel so good I can't stand it," she said.

"I'm hungry." Tim got to his feet.

"There's food on the boat," Rolf said.

"Hey, what's that?" Tim pointed toward tne channel.

Rolf shaded his eyes. "It's a police launch! Quick! They'll see the skiff!"

Tim was running almost as Rolf spoke, tearing across the beach with Brother to grab the skiff's sides and haul it into the trees. The others churned through the water to the sloop. Rolf reached her first, panting and tugging with Mouse and Parry to get the boat farther behind the rocks. Mouse thought she heard a grinding sound under *Windsong*'s hull, but Rolf yelled to keep going. The sloop slid out of sight just as the launch drew even with the entrance to the cove. No one moved. They held their breath. The launch had slowed down, and Rolf climbed up to peek over the rocks. He smelled wet seaweed under his nose, and saw a tiny crab scuttle into a hole beside him. His hands kept slipping, but he dug in his toes and hung on.

"Do you think they know you're here?" Mouse whispered.

"Not yet. I think they're just looking in general." Rolf could see two men on deck, and the noise of the chugging engines drowned out Zec's mewings from the hidden sloop.

Then the engines quieted. The launch was coming almost to a full stop. One minute went by, two, while the men put binoculars to their faces and slowly surveyed the whole channel, sweeping their glasses back around through the palm trees and up the hill. Then, the engines roared, and as quickly as it had come, the launch went past the entrance to the cove and out of sight.

Rolf reached up and swung himself onto the *Windsong*'s deck. Tim and Brother came out of the trees and climbed aboard.

"It's awfully shallow where you've got her," Tim said.

"I know, and I think we hit something. I'm going down to see."

Rolf plunged under and then came back up for his mask. The second time he came up he looked really upset.

"One of the rudder pin bolts is gone," he said. "That rock must have knocked it out."

He took a deep breath and dove again. Tim went down with him, feeling along the rocks. Everyone dove, reaching deep into the slimy cracks. They came up, their lungs bursting, and then went down again. Finally Rolf stopped.

"It's no use. We can't find it."

"How bad is that?" Tim was still gulping air.

"She won't turn without it," Rolf said.

"I've got to get another one right away. I'll have to go to town."

"But you can't!" Mouse protested. "Why can't you go to that other little village?"

"Or we can get it for you," Tim suggested.

Rolf shook his head. "I have to see the bolts — there are a lot of kinds and I can't describe which one you should get."

Parry was fixing a loose string on her bathing suit. "If Brother and I went with you, and you wear a hat, you wouldn't be noticed as much."

Rolf looked at her. "That's not a bad idea." He stood up. "Or a bandana. I've got one in the cabin."

"We'll all go," Tim said. "If anything goes wrong, five people are better than one."

"We can be a gang." Mouse smiled happily. "A gang of Aztecs."

Nine

In the night it rained, and Rolf woke once to hear a thundering downpour on the cabin roof. At sunrise the clouds drifted away, leaving a fresh, washed town and a calm sea, glittering like a blue, jeweled plate.

Mouse, speeding down the road in the car with Captain Fisher, thought the leftover raindrops looked like diamonds, and she was squinting at them through her lashes when the Captain's voice interrupted her.

"Your brother must be happy with that skiff, taking it out so early."

Mouse twisted on the seat, her mind bouncing back to Tim. By now he should be on his way back from the reef, bringing Rolf and Parry and Brother. "He loves it. He never wants to do anything else."

"Well, sunup's certainly a good time for him to catch fish," Captain Fisher said. He slowed the car. "Here we are, the coast road," he announced. "Sure you want to get out?"

Mouse nodded. "I like walking around. "I'll come down to the dock later, when Tim gets back."

She climbed out, trying to look casual as Captain Fisher drove away. She moved across the road and sat down by a wall, her back against the stones. It was still so early hardly any people were around, and Mouse relaxed a little, chewing on a leaf. Her mind wandered, and she listened to some birds twittering in a tree over her head. Donkeys were braying in the field behind her, and dogs barked in houses nearer to town. The air felt soft. She thought about growing up here, even going to school on an island. How marvellous it must be to be here all the time, even when you went to school. She wondered what Rolf's school looked like, before he left it. Then she saw Brother, sauntering toward her along the road.

"We've got a place to hide," he said when he reached her, and she fell into step beside him. They walked across a field and along a back road until they came to some shacks that were covered with tarpaper. Brother pushed open a crazily hung door, and Mouse saw the others crouched inside. They were barely visible in the dim light.

"Did Captain Fisher say anything?" Tim's face peered at her.

"No. He really does think you're fishing." She followed Brother in, feeling her way in the dark.

"What time is it?" Rolf said.

"Seven-thirty," Mouse answered.

"We should wait another fifteen minutes," Parry said.

The central market opened at eight o'clock, and Parry had pointed out that Rolf would be less noticeable if they waited for the crowds, and walked into town with the people who brought produce or came in to work from the surrounding countryside.

Tim stood slowly upright, trying not to hit the top of his head. "Let's decide who's doing what."

"Mouse should go with me," Rolf said. "Without my hair showing, people will think we're the same brother and sister they've been seeing all along. It'd be natural for us to be in a boat supply store."

"Okay," Tim said. "The rest of us can watch the street, and warn you if anyone funny comes." He turned to Mouse. "Stop shoving."

"I can't help it. There's no room in here."

Parry moved suddenly because she thought a bug was running down her back, and upset something on the concrete floor. In the dimness they couldn't see what it was, and they held their breath until the terrible clanking stopped.

"You're standing on my foot." Brother's voice was low. "Parry, get off."

Parry chuckled, a happy sound, Mouse thought. "It felt like a rock," Parry said, and Brother laughed too.

"Shh!" Tim jerked his head. "I hear something."

Instantly Rolf was at the wall, trying to see through a crack. The others dropped silently behind some boxes in the corner. Rolf could see nothing, but now they could all hear men's low voices. They waited, feeling trapped. There was no lock on the door, not even a latch. Rolf looked around for another exit, but there wasn't any, only some wider cracks in the back wall where a little light came in. He peered through there, his eye glued to the wall. He saw brown cloth — it was a man's back, leaning against the shack. He drew back and pointed, his finger to his lips.

"I can't tell." He formed the words silently.

"One's leaning on the shack, one's sitting on the ground."

They crouched again, squashed together and uncomfortable. It was hard not to move. Second after second crept by. Parry wanted to cough. Tim's knee itched. Brother was holding his nose. Suddenly Mouse had an awful feeling of wanting to laugh. She tried to hold it in but it got worse, and she felt she would have to burst or be sick or faint. She felt Tim's hand close on her shoulder, and the feeling stopped immediately. How did he know, she wondered.

The voices fell silent. Rolf left his crack and went to the door. He opened it a half inch, three inches, easing his face out.

"They've gone. I see them walking down the street."

Everyone breathed again, feeling weak.

"What were they doing?"

"Probably just stopping to talk."

"Listen, if they had come in here we wouldn't have known what to do."

"Run."

"Yes, but we should know where to meet." Tim looked at Rolf. "At that big field we came by, with the fig tree."

"Okay." Rolf was getting restless, knotting the bandana on his head. "It's time to go."

They pushed out into bright sunlight. People were coming along the road, and children were running past, yelling and laughing. Suddenly Mouse felt as though school had just let out and they were starting a holiday. Her spirits leaped and she started jogging along beside Rolf.

"I wonder if your picture's posted," she said.

"I doubt it."

Tim was in front with Parry. "They probably only do that in post offices at home."

Brother stopped to pet a brown puppy, and laughed when it licked his face. He tried to pick it up but it wriggled loose and scampered off, and he ran to catch up with the others. Parry was heading for the square, where the steeple clock said nearly eight. People were all around them now, but Mouse noticed Rolf was staying close to the edge of the sidewalk. They turned onto the street along the waterfront, and Parry halted in a doorway.

"From here we better go separate," she said. "And move slow, like you are happy."

Tim walked away toward the docks. Brother slipped across the street into the market stalls.

Parry followed him, and Rolf and Mouse found themselves alone.

"Come on," Rolf said. "It's not far."

They strolled slowly, passing another block. Mouse could see Captain Fisher's warehouses along the water. She saw people going in and out, and Captain Fisher's car parked beside the office building. Rolf was watching the policeman who directed traffic in the square.

"Talk." Rolf smiled at her. "You look scared."

"I am," Mouse said.

It was another half-block to the shop. She tried to talk, but her heart sank when they reached it and the door was closed. Rolf pushed and the door swung open. They walked in and found themselves in a room with counters along the walls. The counters were covered with boxes and there were tables in the center covered with more boxes. The shop owner looked up from a book and stared at them.

"What do you want?" he said.

"We're looking for rudder bolts," Rolf said. The man didn't move. "What size?"

"We're not sure," Mouse said brightly. "We just got here from Chicago, and our father's rented a boat." She turned to Rolf. "He told you, Tim."

"It's a sailboat," Rolf said.

"How big?"

Rolf looked around. "About from there" — he pointed to a wall — "to there, that table."

The man finally got up. "Bolts come in a lot of sizes. Try the boxes on that table, in the middle."

Mouse smiled at him. "Do you think we could buy one or two, and bring them back if they're not right?"

"Yes, if you don't scratch them. It would be better if your father came with you."

"He can't. He has to send a cable about his office."

Rolf was bending over the boxes, picking up bolts and putting them back. After a minute he found the one he wanted, but at Mouse's look he picked out two others. "These look about right," he said, and the man nodded.

They paid as fast as they could and left the shop. Mouse half-expected someone to rush after them, shouting, "Stop!" but no one seemed to be noticing them. She realized she was holding her breath again, and she let it out as they crossed the street and pushed into the crowd in the square. The market was jammed, but Rolf walked briskly through the crowded stalls and out the far side.

"He never suspected a thing," Mouse gloated.

"Right." Rolf's voice sounded tense. They weren't safe yet.

They walked faster, into a serious-looking street that had a bank and a government building with a flag.

"Parry and Brother are following us," Rolf said.

Mouse turned and saw them, well back, but definitely following. She felt lighthearted with relief.

"Look at all those offices. Imagine being shut up in one." She ran her finger along the bricks as they passed a building. "What really happens in offices? I have never understood what grown people do."

"I'm not sure, they fool with paper. But I wouldn't sit down like that all the time. I'd never be anything but an explorer, on boats."

"Mmn."

At the top of the street Rolf zigzagged, cutting behind a church to another street, and then another. Finally they turned around. Parry and Brother weren't in sight. This was almost a lane, cobblestoned and peaceful. Rolf stopped and caught Mouse by the arm. "Look. Chickens."

She saw them across the way, pecking in the gutter.

"I'm going to try and buy a couple."

"Now?" She looked around, feeling nervous again. "Do you think this is a good time?"

"Yes. Go sit over there, keep watch." He pointed to a barrel under a rain pipe. "And try to look normal." His grin flickered.

She glanced up and down the lane, but there was no one moving. Parry and Brother still weren't in sight. She went and sat, and watched Rolf go up to a house behind a fence. A woman came out of the house, and Mouse saw Rolf talking to her. She thought of fried chicken and her mouth watered. She noticed two men had turned into the street farther up and were strolling slowly her way.

"Stop dreaming." Rolf's voice made her jump. He was standing in front of her, smiling, and under his arm were two chickens. "Fine lookout you are."

"But how . . ."

"Not now. Hurry." He found a cardboard box in a pile of trash and put the chickens in it, punching holes with his knife. Mouse leaned over and peered through the holes. She saw a moving grey thing with a white streak and she heard muffled clucks.

"It's not very big in there," she said.

"They're all right," Rolf said, straightening up.

A hand fell on his back.

For an instant shock kept him from moving — he saw only the street and the sky. Then a man's voice said, "Where did you get those chickens?" and Rolf twisted around, loosening the man's grip.

"I bought them." Rolf planted his feet. "What business is it of yours?"

"That's my house, that's what business it is," the man said. "And you've got two of my chickens in that box."

"The lady in there sold them to me," Rolf said.

"She's got no right to do that," the man said. "If she really did."

He looked mean. Mouse eased slowly back, hoping they wouldn't notice her. She edged along the cobblestones, reached a bush, slid behind it, and backed into the yard of the next house as the man was almost pushing Rolf up to the front porch.

"We'll ask her," Mouse heard him say. "Come on."

Rolf was trapped. The other man was behind him. At the front door the first man banged on the door. "Edna, come out," he called.

There was no answer. He went inside. Rolf and the second man waited on the porch. The box was getting heavy and Rolf put it down.

"Look," he said, "I paid for these chickens, but if she's left and you don't believe me, you can have them back."

"Oh, no you don't," the first man said. "Too many things getting stole around this neighborhood. Now we've caught you, you aren't getting away. I'm going for the constable."

Before Rolf could move the man caught his arm, and with a shove he was through the door and into the house. "You're staying here with Tom till I get back," he said.

Mouse ran. Where were Parry and Brother? They must be somewhere. Probably they'd seen the men and stayed out of sight.

"Parry," Mouse said loudly.

"Here." Parry's head appeared over a low pink wall. "Brother's gone for Tim."

They heard a gate slam and Mouse shot over the wall. The man who had said he was getting the constable was striding their way.

"Where's the police station?" Mouse whispered.

"Back at the square," Parry said. "Brother won't be able to find Tim in time. We'll have to do something ourselves."

The man went by and disappeared. They slid over the wall and scuttled up the street to the fence. The man called Tom was visible in the doorway, but Rolf was not in sight. They ducked down.

Inside, Rolf was sitting in a chair in a dark, gloomy room. Two windows in the back were closed from the outside by heavy wooden shutters. Probably hooked shut from the outside too, Rolf thought. There was no other exit, and Rolf turned back to examine the furniture. Maybe he could find a weapon. He eyed some shelves standing along a wall piled with fishing gear, and saw a spearhead and a shark hook. He got up and wandered across the room, pretending to be bored. Tom looked up briefly from his seat and went back to contemplating his hands in his lap. Rolf yawned and started back to the chair, angling past the bookcase. His hand slid out, his fingers closed on the shark hook and he slid it in his pocket.

Someone shrieked outside. Tom jumped. The sound came again. "*Ahhh, ow-w-w.*"

Tom got up and peered at the yard through the door. Now it was louder, a steady wailing. Parry was lying on the dirt inside the gate, banging on the ground with her fist. Tom went out on the porch. "What's the matter?" He didn't sound friendly.

Her only answer was a loud moan. Tom walked to the steps, glancing back at the room. Rolf was sprawled in a chair, looking nearly asleep. Tom went down the walk toward Parry. He bent over her, asking her what the matter was.

"My leg, my leg!" she wailed.

At one of the back shutters Rolf heard a knock and a scraping sound. It lifted, and then fell back with a bang. Rolf leaped for it, pushing out and up.

"Hurry," Mouse panted outside. "It's heavy."

She was standing on a box, and Rolf slid his leg out and landed beside her, easing the shutter down again. They could hear Parry, still crying loudly.

"We'd better make sure she gets away." Rolf jumped off the box and headed for the corner of the house.

"No. She said to run." Mouse had started the other way. "Back here. There's a gate."

They dashed through the yard and into a

vacant lot behind the cottage next door. A high board fence stood at the far end of that, and below lay another street.

"Do you know where Tim and Brother are?" Rolf leaped at the fence.

"Yes."

The top of the boards hit Mouse in the stomach and she grunted. She tried again, kicking, and scrambled over. She landed beside Rolf in the street below. They jogged, trying to look normal, pacing themselves around a corner, down an alley, and into another street.

"Where's everybody else?" Rolf's words came out with his breath.

"Parry's getting them. They'll meet us at the fig tree."

"If she gets away." Rolf was still worried.

It seemed to Mouse that the edge of town was much farther than it had been coming in, but finally they came to the field and flung themselves down under the fig tree, panting.

"That was smart, what you and Parry did," Rolf said.

Mouse dabbed with a fig leaf at a bleeding scratch on her knee. "We had to do something. And it was Parry's idea. I never would have known about those shutters, or about standing on that box."

Rolf heard a noise and sat up. Parry and Brother were trotting toward them, waving.

"Did you get the bolt?" Tim was right behind them.

"Yes."

"Let's go, then." Tim grinned. "I'm starving. I never got any breakfast."

They found the skiff untouched where they had left it, under some sea grape branches at the beach. Tim kept the engine at full throttle in spite of the load, drenching everyone with spray, but no one cared. The sun was a midsummer furnace, and the spray kept them cool. They splashed ashore at the little island and Brother pranced up the beach. "That trip was a lot of fun," he said.

Rolf pulled the bolts from his pocket, starting toward the rocks and the sloop. "But it was too risky," he said. "I've got to fix the rudder and leave."

Mouse noticed that his voice sounded flat, and she had a sudden feeling that he didn't really want to go.

"How long have you been planning to go to Mexico?" Tim asked.

"Ever since I was little. At least my father

has. He was just waiting for me to get big enough to go with him. He was interested in archaeology and stuff, and he wanted to show me all the Aztec ruins, and the Mayans in Yucután, and everything."

Rolf slowed down, and Mouse turned to look at him.

"He died this winter," Rolf said.

Their minds spun. Died. No one could think of anything to say.

"I'm going anyway, though." Rolf was almost talking to himself. "I think he'd want me to." His voice trailed off.

"But it's not safe," Parry said. "You shouldn't do it alone."

"Yes, I should. I know the whole route. I can do it." Rolf reached the sloop and swung aboard. "Anyway, now the constable is after me too, because of the chickens." He squared his shoulders. "There's no way I can turn back now."

Ten

"Well." Tim broke the silence. "The first thing to do is fix the rudder. We'll help you."

Rolf looked relieved. "Okay. I can do the underwater part, but if you hold the shaft, and someone else hands me tools overboard..."

"Me." Brother climbed onto the deck.

"We should keep watch, so nobody surprises us this time," Parry said.

"Right." Tim climbed on board. "After we eat." He grinned. "I'm starving, remember?"

Rolf reached into a locker and held up a can of tomato soup. "Sandwich insides. It drips, but it's good."

He got bread from below and they ate sitting on the cabin roof. Slowly the conversation got back to normal, but under it everyone was thinking about what Rolf had told them.

"Have you got good navigation stuff?" Tim asked.

"Enough," Rolf answered. "And I know how to use the stars."

Tim remembered when he had been almost jealous of Rolf, because of all the things Rolf knew. Now all he felt was worried.

"Maybe we could spend the night over here before you go," Mouse was saying, "have a sort of farewell dinner, or something. We could help you with the boat if anything else goes wrong."

"Nothing will," Rolf said. "But spending the night's a good idea."

Mouse looked at Tim. "Captain Fisher'd probably be relieved to have us out of the house. Don't you think?"

"It's worth a try." Tim got up and picked up the wrenches.

Rolf put on the face mask and lowered himself over the side, and Parry and Mouse dove in too. The girls swam slowly to the cove's entrance and pushed under the mangrove branches, staring out at the channel. They could hear the boys' voices behind them, floating across the water.

"I still don't think Rolf should go," Parry said. "His boat's fine, but the weather's getting chancy. And it's too far."

"But he has to," Mouse said. "I'd do it too,

164

if that had happened in our family." The thought made her stomach lurch. "I wonder where his mother is."

Parry frowned. "I was thinking the same thing. I was wondering if he has one."

"Umn."

Few boats were in the bay, and Mouse noticed clouds building up in the west, high and deep. It looked as though it was going to rain again. She thought of Rolf, sailing south, and she tried to imagine the days here without him. She couldn't. I want to go with him, she thought. Then she shook her head. It would be too lonely.

"I wish there was some way to change everything," she said aloud.

"That's what Granpa's always saying, to change things you don't like. But I can't think of any way we can change what's happened to Rolf."

"Neither can I."

They sat for a time in silence, watching the rain clouds pile higher. Most of the boats were turning in.

"That cloud's worse than yesterday," Parry said. "I wonder if the boys see it."

"They must be nearly done by now. Let's go back."

Rolf came up from under the stern just as Mouse and Parry reached the sloop, his expression almost cheerful. "I think it's fixed. We can test it when the boats have gone in."

"They've gone in now," Mouse said. "Look."

"Jeeps!" Tim straightened up and looked at the sky.

"It's only rain," Parry said. "There's no wind with it. The windy squalls are the scary ones."

Even so, this was not like the other showers they had seen, drifting across the island to spill their loads and pass quickly on. This rain had dropped over the main island like a gray curtain, and now it was moving across the bay in a solid wall.

"Let's go up to the mill and get a good look," Rolf said.

They ran up the meadow and puffed to the roof of the tower. They watched the rain come closer and closer, and then, when it reached them, it was as if the bottom had dropped out of a sea above their heads. Water fell in sheets from the sky, blotting out the bay, the cove, even each other's faces in the silver deluge.

"Go down under the shelf," Rolf shouted

over the roar of falling water. They ran downstairs and huddled together, soaking wet.

"Suppose we get stuck here, and the bay begins to rise." Tim was scaring himself. "Up into the cove, over the beach, coming up the meadow . . ."

"But it won't," Parry said. She squatted calmly on her heels, making little mounds of dirt on the floor and smoothing them out again with a sweep of her palm. "I like the rain, it cools me off. I got a heat stroke once," she added.

Mouse squatted beside her. "What happened?"

"It was after I stayed on the beach too long looking for shells," Parry said. "I slept — for three days, while Granpa put water cloths on my head. Then I woke up, and it was gone."

Mouse thought. "It must have been a funny feeling to sleep for three days."

Brother was wandering back along the wall, poking his fingers in between the stones. "Mouse, look behind you."

She turned and saw a huge, hideous crab edging slowly out of the shadows.

"Get it away, get it away!" she shrieked and leaped sideways, landing on Tim.

"Ow, get off!" he shouted.

"It's only a land crab," Brother laughed, while Rolf went after it with a stick. The creature, about the size of a small cat, backed slowly away, its front claws waving menacingly at them all.

"I'm not afraid of it, really." Mouse felt ashamed of her shrieks.

"You are," Tim said, "you're shaking like jelly."

Sunlight suddenly fell across Rolf's face through a hole in the wall. He walked to the door. "The rain's stopping," he said.

Outside a million wet drops were sparkling in the light, and parts of the sky were deep blue again.

"That's really fast," Mouse said, looking at the disappearing rain clouds. "It's just gone."

Rolf took a stance, his legs wide, and threw back his head. " 'Till yonder cloud . . . good hunting! . . . loose; the rain that breaks our water truce.' " He jumped at Mouse and grabbed her arm. "The truce is over, the truce is over!" he said in a singsong voice.

She stared at him. "But that's from *The Jungle Book*! I didn't know you knew it! I mean . . ." She stopped in confusion.

"I know a lot of things I never say." He grinned, and started down the hill through the rain-soaked grass. The others caught up with him at the cove, and Zec rose squawking to greet them, flapping his wings against Rolf's head and beaking his hair.

Tim pulled the skiff out of its hiding place. "It's too late to test the rudder now. How about waiting till tomorrow, so we can sail with you?"

Rolf nodded. "Get here as early as you can, though."

"And we'll bring a lot of food, if we can stay," Mouse said. "Maybe a cake, and a lot of Cokes and stuff."

"You know," she added on the way back to town, "Rolf hasn't actually said when he's leaving. If we just don't talk about it he might stay even longer."

"Yeah, but if he's going, he'd better not wait too long," Tim said. "The weather's really getting worse. If that rain today had wind with it, I'd have hated to see it."

No one was around when they docked at the wharfs, and when Captain Fisher finally got home, he hardly seemed to hear Tim say that they wanted to spent the night out. He did ask where they planned to camp, but only nodded casually when Tim said on the beach.

"I got a letter from your father this morning," he said abruptly. "They have to stay longer than they thought, another week or so. I told them you're no trouble here."

"Well, thanks," Tim said. "And you don't mind if we spend the night out, then?"

"No, take what you need and don't let the sand crabs bite." Captain Fisher chuckled and walked into the den. Then he came back. "Sure you're all right, now? Getting enough to eat, all that? Not bored?"

"Oh, no, we're not bored," Mouse said. "We're having a lovely time."

"Yes, well." Captain Fisher sounded vague as he disappeared into the library. "Let me know if you need anything." His words trailed after him.

"Sometimes I don't understand him." Mouse started for the storeroom.

"What do you mean?"

"It's like he's not noticing us, and yet before, when we wanted to do stuff, he was super careful."

"Yeah. Well, he's busy with the election." Tim pulled open the kitchen door. "He told us he's all wrapped up in it."

"Maybe so, but I still think something's weird."

Tim stopped. It was unusual for Mouse to be worried. "What do you mean?"

"I don't know." She looked at him. "I just have a feeling we ought to be really careful, that's all."

That night a strong breeze came up, sweeping and fidgeting around the house, flinging salt air in the doorways and open places.

"Probably a squall somewhere far off," Mrs. Shaw said at supper.

"Do you think it'll be a hurricane?" Tim asked.

"Not yet," the housekeeper said. "But the time's coming."

The wind kept up all night, and it was still blowing the next morning on the way to town. It lifted Mouse's hair while she walked to the bakery, and blew the cooler top right off while Tim lugged the heavy box across the wharf. The water slapped against the pilings, joggling the skiff while Mouse untied the line. They fought little waves all the way across to the reef, and white clouds scudded fast in the sky. At the cove, the *Windsong* was tugging on her anchor, straining to follow the wind.

"It's a good sea to test the rudder," Rolf greeted them. "Choppy. Captain Fisher's boats will work close to shore where it's calm.

So we'll go out to sea." He smiled. "Her first big test in the open ocean."

"That'll be great," Tim said. "Where are Parry and Brother?"

"They can't sail. Granpa went out in the dinghy, and he left them some work. They'll be here tonight. Can you stay?"

Mouse nodded. "Captain Fisher didn't mind at all. I told you he wouldn't. And we've got a lot of food."

"That's good," Rolf grinned. "We'll be starved by tonight, from sailing."

He hauled up the sails, and Mouse got the anchor up. Tim let go his sheet and the foresail swung over the water, flopping crazily. In a minute it filled out, and almost before they knew it they were in the channel, racing along the reef. In no time they were opposite the narrow opening through the reef, and Rolf brought the sloop into the wind and headed for it. Mouse caught her breath and watched the jagged coral coming at them, boiling waves hitting the outside with sucking, slapping sounds. Tim ran to the bow, his eyes on the rocks. He pointed left, then straight, then right. In seconds they were through the passage. They shot onto big choppy waves that went even faster than the sloop, sliding out in

172

front of her bow and racing on toward the horizon.

Rolf put the boat on a broad reach. The windward deck went up as the boat heeled over, but she held steady and settled into rushing before the wind.

"The rudder's working perfectly," he called. "We're doing fine."

Behind, the dinghy bounced from side to side at the end of its line, sliding and smacking in the *Windsong*'s boiling wake. Farther back, the town looked like small grey boulders on the main island. Dark patches — cloud shadows — seemed to shift and leap across the hazy green light of its rain forests.

Tim took the helm. He moved the tiller carefully. In his mind he listed the things Rolf had taught him before he brought the *Windsong* about, sheeting in the mainsail and jib, pushing the tiller firmly to leeward, calling, "Ready about."

Rolf waved approval while the bow came into the wind and the sails flapped, then filled. The boat surged ahead, pointing west again.

Mouse went forward. The water slammed over the bow, soaking her hair and her bathing suit. She edged onto the bowsprit, riding it up and down like a galloping horse as the sloop careened through the waves. She held on tight and turned around to wave at Tim and Rolf. They were standing under the billowing mainsail, and she laughed at Tim's hair, standing straight up in the wind.

Suddenly her arm fell. Behind them, racing through the waves, came a black motor launch. Across the wind came the unmistakable sound of a motor siren. Mouse shouted and waved frantically, but the boys only smiled at her and waved back. Then she pointed, and they turned around. She saw Rolf leap to the helm, shouting something at Tim, who rushed for the cabin. Rolf swung the sloop to leeward so hard that the rigging groaned, and the gunwale ploughed under the foaming waves. The boom slung wildly across the deck, and Mouse saw the bucket go, spinning crazily into the water and out of sight behind them. Tim shot from the cabin with an armload of canvas.

"Quick!" he shouted, racing to the mast to put up a larger jib. Mouse sprang to help him loosen a rope and thread it through the rings. The new sail billowed out and the *Windsong* leaped ahead, almost as though she were flying. Mouse caught hold of a stay, hanging on with all her strength.

Tim could see men on the launch's deck. To his horror he realized one was Captain Fisher, waving a megaphone.

"Get down!" Tim yelled in Mouse's ear. "Don't let him see us!"

She dropped to the deck. Her skin felt numb from spray, and their speed made the wind burn her face. She put her head down and felt her heart thump. Suddenly Tim grabbed her arm.

"There's Granpa!" he shouted.

Mouse twisted around. Granpa's dinghy was off to port, close to the reef. She could see him sitting, erect and dignified, and while she was watching, the black launch began to turn aside. It slowed down, and then it started to circle back.

"They're after him too!" Mouse moaned.

"Get the binoculars!" Rolf shouted. "They're below."

Tim slid down for them and steadied himself to focus on the launch. By now it was pulling up alongside Granpa, and then it stopped, the two boats rocking together on the waves. Tim saw Captain Fisher lean over to talk to Granpa, who still sat calmly in the dinghy. The two men seemed engrossed in conversation. Captain Fisher kept pointing toward the mangrove's islands. Finally he stepped back and the launch's propellers foamed behind her as she cut loose and swung away from the dinghy. He raised his hand to Granpa in a kind of salute, then sat down as the launch turned in a tight circle and headed back the way she had come. Granpa's little outboard started up too, and he took up a meandering course along the reef.

"What's going on?" Tim demanded. "They've quit chasing us! And Granpa too."

Rolf had never slackened speed, but now he handed Tim the tiller and turned to study the rapidly diminishing boats.

"I don't know," he said slowly. "That's really queer."

Tim stood up. The sloop was going like a wild thing, and he was having trouble holding her steady. Rolf took the tiller back again.

"Granpa's okay, anyway. We can ask him later what they said. Right now I'm getting out of here."

He sheeted in the mainsail until the sloop was on a broad reach again, running straight south. Soon Granpa's dinghy was only a black dot behind them, and they were opposite the western arm of the bay, tearing through long, sweeping waves off the huge point of land.

Once around it, Rolf seemed relax. They were far off-shore, and the island lay off to port like a large green hump, a dinosaur's hump, Mouse thought. She stretched out on the cabin roof, listening to the wind moan and hum through the rigging. The water was deep-blue and the big ocean swells seemed to roll in from far beyond the horizon. Mouse's mind followed them, imagining farther and farther until it got too much to think about. All at once she understood how Rolf must feel about sailing. The sea went everywhere, and the *Windsong* could follow it, sailing day after day through the spray and the sunlight, even all over the world.

"I'm never going back to Chicago," she said aloud, but the boys were talking and they didn't hear. She got up and moved into the cockpit.

"Can you imagine how mad Captain Fisher'd be if he'd known we were on this boat?" she said.

"I don't like to think about it," Tim said. He turned to Rolf. "What's our plan?"

"We'll hide someplace down here till the sun gets low," Rolf said. "Then we'll sail back and have our Aztec party." He smiled at Mouse and she giggled.

He watched the shoreline until he found a splash of white that meant a beach. When he saw what he wanted, he came about and tacked toward it. The white came closer and closer until it became a deserted lagoon. Rolf headed in, and the sloop glided across the quiet surface. The anchor went out with a loud splash and sank in pale, lovely water. The sun was hot, sheltered from the wind, and on shore the palms were gently waving. Seabirds cried and flew around the boat, almost tame.

Mouse leaned over the rail. "I feel as though I'm still moving."

Rolf laughed. "Those are sea legs." He swung down the companionway and came back with canned sardines and bananas. "There's only one sure way to cure them."

Mouse stared at him. "What?"

He grinned, and peeled off his shirt. "Go swimming," he said.

They sailed back late in the afternoon. The wind was nearly gone and the sea was calm. Rolf stayed far offshore to take advantage of a westerly breeze, and only headed in when they were opposite the mangrove islands. Tim and Mouse posted themselves on either side of the bow and guided him through the reef passage, coming into the channel just at Granpa's beach.

"There's his dinghy," Tim said.

"And there he is."

Parry and Brother were with Granpa. They were waving. Rolf dropped anchor in four feet of water and waded ashore.

"Welcome," Granpa called.

They nodded, suddenly uncertain. Even in the fading light Granpa didn't seem like a man they could rush up to and demand to know what had happened that morning.

"You are a fine sailor," Granpa said to Rolf. "You gave that launch a run this morning."

"Why did they turn back?" Rolf said. "They must have recognized my boat. And they didn't seem to bother you either."

"They turned aside because Captain Fisher had an urgent message for me," Granpa said.

Rolf stood squarely and Mouse thought he seemed to grow an inch. "I don't understand," he said. "Parry told us you were . . ."

"Keeping out of sight?" Granpa smiled. "Yes. But not from Captain Fisher. He is an old friend."

Granpa put his hand on Rolf's shoulder.

"What matters is that they turned back, isn't it? And you can have your banquet. We've even made conch chowder, if you'd like some."

"And Brother and I cleaned up the mill," Parry said. "So we can eat there if you want to. We built a fire inside, too, in case it rains."

Rolf looked at Parry, and the conch chowder. Granpa chuckled suddenly.

"If you don't take it, I will," he said. "I love conch chowder."

"So do I," Rolf said. He stepped back, but he still looked tense. "We can share it," he said finally. "Will you eat with us?"

Granpa shook his head. "No. Thanks. This is your party." He sounded serious again. "But there is something I want you to know . . . I think what you are doing takes courage. I want you to remember that."

Rolf stared at him. "Thanks," he said. Then he took a deep breath and turned to the others. "Tim and I should take *Windsong* to the cove and hide her, and get the rest of the food. We can meet up there."

Brother decided to go with them, and Granpa waded out to push them off. Mouse and Parry picked up the chowder pail and walked through the trees in the sunset.

"It was a great idea you had about the mill," Mouse said. "At last we get to use our hideout."

"Except Brother and I've changed it," Parry said. "I hope you like what we did."

When Mouse walked through the door of the mill she couldn't believe her eyes. Flowers hung up and down the walls and poked out between the stones. Vines, planted in big tin cans, cascaded from the shelf. A huge old millstone sat in the middle of the room, covered with more flowers, tin plates, and cups. Shiny green mats, made of woven palm fronds, lay on the floor. There were even two hammocks strung across a corner, with a bucket of flowers in between.

"I was worried because we did it without you," Parry said.

"It's perfect," Mouse said.

She walked slowly around, staring at everything, and stopped in front of a large and astonishing shell figure that rose from a pile of stones — a statue, modelled after the one in the library Aztec book. It was four feet tall, and Parry's best conch shells stuck sideways from its head, like big bat ears. It was the first thing Rolf saw when the boys came in.

"Oh, great," he said. "Teocalli!"

Brother chuckled. "Whoever he is, he sure took a lot of shells."

"How do you know it's a he?" Mouse said. "It might be a girl."

Parry laughed and lit the candles, and Tim lit the fire. Light flickered magically around the room, glowing on the polished stone walls and the flowers. Mouse sat down, stirring the chowder over the fire. The others unloaded the cooler and spread out the rest of the food.

"I'm starving," Mouse said happily. "And we have everything we need to be a lost tropical family."

"Except a way back to our lost homeland," Tim said in a fake accent. He was pulling out ham, avocados, tomatoes, Cokes, bread, butter, and cake. Besides the chowder, Parry and Brother contributed plantains and yams, and Rolf had brought pineapples, oysters, and a fruit called pawpaw. They arranged it all on the table, with the hot chowder in the middle.

"Should we start?"

"Yes," Rolf said.

Everyone sat down on the mats, piling food on their plates and dipping into the chowder with the cups.

"It's good," Tim said.

"What did you expect?" Parry said.

Tim looked sheepish. "I wasn't sure what conch would taste like."

"I need some butter." Parry struggled to open Rolf's pocket knife.

"Here." Rolf grabbed some hunks of bread.

"I want tomatoes." Brother dumped them in his bowl.

"I like not having manners," Mouse said. She rolled over, chewing with her mouth open. "Teocalli's hungry too."

Parry giggled. "I'll take her a plate."

"Actually, we should call it a sacrifice," Rolf said.

"Gross. Is that really what they did?" Tim reached for a huge yam.

"Well" — Rolf loaded his plate again — "yes. But they had fair laws about it. And anyway they had another legend, about a tall man who came from across the sea. He talked about being good, but he had to leave. The book didn't say why. They believed his heart became the morning star."

"Cripes, I wonder what our fine at the library is by now," Tim said.

"You aren't listening." Mouse liked the morning star part and sometimes Tim didn't seem to care about anything.

"I was. Rolf said a man came from across the sea in the morning. Maybe that's why everybody wishes on the evening star. It got mixed up after such a long time."

"Shut up."

Parry looked at the table, feeling full of food and warm and lazy. "We've eaten everything but the peanut butter."

Rolf unscrewed the top. "We could play darts with it." He handed a glob to everyone and started throwing, aiming at a place on the wall. Their shots went everywhere, hitting the stones, the floor, even sailing out the window. They threw backward and over their shoulders and from flat on the floor, whooping and shouting and throwing until the target was so covered with peanut butter no one could tell whose shot was whose, and it was impossible to know who was winning.

Finally Brother lay still, his face in the dirt. "I like that game."

Tim jumped to his feet. "Let's go up on the roof."

They clattered up, carrying the candles. The breeze had died, and the island was very quiet, the air feeling soft against their cheeks. The hurricane lamp flickered on their bare brown arms and legs and shone in their eyes. Rolf leaned over and blew it out, and they could see better. He pointed.

"Look. Lightning."

They all looked. "A storm?" Tim said.

"A squall. It's a long way off, though."

Now they all saw the vivid streaks that slashed across the black sky to the east. They were too far away to hear thunder, but it was an oddly frightening sight, like seeing a terrible fight from too far away to help, and not being able to hear the people shouting.

They were silent, their faces turned up to the huge sky, watching, wondering, listening to the breathing night — the grass, the palm trees, an occasional clink as a pebble dropped to the shelf from the roof, a rustle that might have been a rat. Brother saw a falling star.

"They bring good luck," Parry said.

"I hope so," Mouse said. "Did you ever hear of somebody named Amelia Earhart?"

"No."

"She was a woman pilot a long time ago. Dad told me about it. She tried to fly across the Pacific in one of those little planes."

As soon as she said it Mouse wished she hadn't, because the part that had popped into her mind was that Amelia Earhart had disappeared, and no one had ever seen her again.

"What happened?" Tim was asking.

"I don't remember," Mouse said hastily. "She was famous anyway."

Brother yawned. "I'm getting sleepy."

"Me too," Rolf said. "Let's go down to the boat."

He lit the candle and they trooped down the steps, the firelight throwing weird shadows up in their faces. They threw the food scraps outside and packed up the cooler, working in sleepy silence. Rolf was about to put out the fire when he stopped.

"We need names," he said. "Aztec names. So we'll remember who we are."

He ran his finger across a glob of peanut butter that was still stuck to the wall. He walked over to Tim and smeared it on his forehead.

"Your name is Kayab," he said. "The swimmer."

He touched everybody — Parry was Pax, the shell collector, Brother was Zip, the diver, and Mouse was Hut, the dreamer. "I'll be Vaca, the sailor."

"You're making those names up," Brother said.

"It doesn't matter," Rolf said. "Just never forget them. And never forget tonight."

"We won't," Mouse said. "Not ever."

Then Tim put out the fire, and they went out into the moon-drenched meadow and walked down the hill to the boat.

Eleven

Tim was the first person awake. For a minute he couldn't remember where he was, but then he heard a curlew cry, flying low over the water, and he sat up, realizing he was on the *Windsong*'s deck. The sun was moving slowly up to the horizon, throwing coloured clouds above it, and flocks of birds rushed up from the beach into the sky and down again, skimming the water and sending showers of drops in the air.

Tim got up and picked his way across the deck, stepping over the others' sleeping forms. He leaned over and stuck one toe into the water; it felt warm. He lowered himself over the side and dropped in. The water felt good and he woke all the way up. He swam around the boat, keeping his strokes under the surface so his splashes wouldn't wake the others. A school of tiny fish flashed by him, and he thought of trying to catch a fish for breakfast.

He climbed back aboard to get Rolf's net and saw Brother roll over.

"What time is it?" Brother asked.

"I don't know," Tim whispered. "Want to come fishing?"

Brother shook his head. "I'm still asleep."

Tim nodded and crept off to find the fins and the mask and the net, and lower himself in again feet first. The fins made his strokes strong and fast and took him rapidly to the mouth of the cove, where he stopped, treading water. The water out in the channel seemed calmer than usual, and Tim decided to look for fish there. The fins would help him if there was a current, especially below the surface.

He put his face down and saw a few small porgies idling under him, but they weren't big enough to bother with. He went under and rolled over on his back to watch the chain of his air bubbles, rising silver to the gently moving mirror of the surface. He wondered why he couldn't see the sky, and then he realized that the sun was reflecting on the water.

He popped up for air and went down again. Ahead, a shallow underwater trench angled out toward the reefs, strewn with big boulders and waving plants. Tim swam into the ravine, exploring a tunnel between the largest rocks. Fish were streaking away in front of him, and some of them were good-sized. His breath ran out and he backed out of the tunnel and popped to the surface. He could see the sloop, lying quietly on her anchor line. There was no sign of life on her decks, so they must still be asleep. Tim took big gulps of air and plunged down again, into the tunnel again. It narrowed, and the rocks almost closed above him. A big yellow snapper came out of no-where, a perfect size for breakfast. It darted ahead and Tim kicked after it, fast. He pushed the net forward. Another kick. His net shot out. He had it! He flipped the handle hard and twirled the net shut. Elated, he swivelled around to swim out.

Then he recoiled. A torpedo-shaped fish with rows of teeth hung motionless in the water at the entrance to the tunnel. It was nearly five feet long, and Tim recognized it from pictures he had seen — a barracuda.

He tried to remember what Rolf had said about the difference between barracudas and sharks that attacked moving objects, and left the motionless ones alone? Or was it barracudas?

Because he had to move. His lungs were

beginning to ache, and he had to get to the surface for air. Straining, he raised his face. He saw an opening in the narrow space between the rocks above, and he thrust upward, kicking hard. He grabbed the rocks with one hand and pulled himself up into the opening. He pushed the net through above him and squeezed one shoulder after it, his skin scraping on the rough edges. Fear made his legs tingle beneath him. Where was the creature, how close had it come? He tried not to imagine its tearing rush . . . coming through the gulf beneath him . . . and then both of his shoulders slid through. Two kicks and he was on the surface, gulping air. He pushed up his mask and looked around. Brother was coming out of the cove and swimming toward him.

"Get back!" Tim yelled. "There's a barracuda somewhere around here!"

"Try to find it!" Brother shouted back. "Splash the water. I'm coming!"

He put his head down and swam faster, and Tim pulled on his mask and looked under the surface.

The fish was there. Somehow it had found him again, and now it was closer, still hanging like a motionless log in the water. When did it swim? Tim thought. Could barracudas be that slow-moving? But as he turned toward Brother, out of the corner of his eyes he saw the fish shoot toward him like a rocket. He stopped, and it stopped too, its body again totally still. Tim felt a pang of terror. What was it up to? Its ugly shape looked bigger, and its jutting teeth seemed almost like a sinister smile.

He saw the empty net floating on the surface about ten yards off. He thrashed toward it, kicking as hard as he could. His legs felt heavy, and he wished he didn't have the fins on. His hand closed on the net's handle just as Brother reached his side.

"Over there," Tim panted. "At least I think it's there."

Brother went under and came up quickly. "Yep. But I think he's only watching us. They're very curious fish." He took the net and moved it in a half circle on the surface in front of him, pushing hard against the water's resistance. The big fish backed off, but then it began to circle. It wouldn't go away. When Brother stopped moving the net, the fish suddenly moved toward them again.

"Do they attack people?" Tim and Brother were close together, kicking.

"They will, but they're not like sharks —

they don't just come for no reason." Brother was out of breath and his words came out in heaves. "We'll have to rush him. Stay with me."

Tim nodded, marvelling at Brother's calm tone. Brother was such a little kid, but he was braver than anyone Tim had ever seen.

"Go."

They dove, and Brother headed straight toward the fish. He held the net in front of him, jabbing and thrusting, waving his arms. The fish backed off. Now they could really see the way the barracuda moved — in short bursts of speed, stopping to hang motionless in the water and watch them. Brother zipped to the surface and went down again, jabbing. This time he came close enough to hit the barracuda in the side. The fish flashed away sideways, came back, circled, and then suddenly it was gone.

They waited, not certain. They needed air, and went up. It was still gone.

"Yowee," Brother breathed. "That was some big fish."

"He sure was," Tim said. "But you got him off."

"I never saw one that big before," Brother said. "It scared me."

"Me too," Tim said. "Let's get to shore."

They swam back to the cove, keeping their faces in and looking all around the sea under them. But nothing was there except waving sea grass and beams of sunlight, and when they reached the cove entrance Tim slowed down again.

"I had a really good snapper in the net before the barracuda showed up," he said.

Brother spouted water. "There might be some over by those mangrove trees — that's the kind of place they like."

Tim nodded. They floated closer to the trees which grew in the water at the island's edge. Brother was right — a whole school of mutton snappers waved in the current just offshore. Tim floated up from the far side, hardly moving, while Brother scooted around to wait under the trees. Now Tim heard noises from the sloop. He heard Mouse laugh and then a loud splash, but he didn't look up — he was concentrating too hard.

"Pssst!" Brother pointed.

One big fish had headed out from the rest. Slowly, inch by inch, Tim moved the net forward. He pushed down, hard. The fish hit the net, but Tim was quick and turned it sideways to close the opening. The net coiled in his hands, but Tim held on.

"You got a good one!" Brother exulted.

Brother took it from the net and Tim followed the school, which had merely moved a little way along the trees. They caught two more before the school passed, and Tim felt elated. He had met a barracuda, the scariest thing he could think of, and caught three snappers too. He suddenly realized that if he hadn't had a slim build he couldn't have squeezed through that hole in the rocks, or eased his way between the mangrove roots.

"We're going to have a great breakfast," he said to Brother.

"Right." Brother headed into the cove.

When they climbed aboard the *Windsong*, Rolf and Mouse were still yawning themselves awake, but Parry was up and she looked upset.

"I hope you were careful. You know barracuda are still out at sunrise."

"We were," Brother chuckled.

"Very." Tim grinned.

Brother laid the fish out on the cabin top, because cleaning them in the water might attract the barracuda back or even a shark. Tim tried to copy the way Brother drew his knife right under the spiny bones in one movement, then made another skillful line that lifted out the big fillets.

Rolf found some leftover butter and fried them on the primus, and Parry added big chunks of banana to the pan. When it was ready Brother squeezed lime juice all over everything. Someone got the leftover cake from the cooler, and everyone sat down.

"Yum," Mouse announced. "I like it."

She walked around the deck, chewing, sloshing a mop and a pail of water in front of her.

"Get every board, every crack clean." Rolf helped himself to more fish.

"You sound like some kind of dictator," Mouse said.

"About my boat, I am." He grinned. "But do a good job and I'll release your leader."

"Who's my leader?" Mouse said. "Brother?"

"No, Zec. He's a prince, disguised as a sea gull." Rolf threw the gull in the air, and Tim laughed. He thought about how back at home nobody could say something like that without sounding weird, and here it seemed perfectly natural. He watched Zec flap off and Mouse empty the bucket on Rolf. Tim put his foot out lazily as Rolf ran by and tripped him headlong into the water, and Mouse and Parry jumped in too, and Tim and Brother followed, shouting.

They had climbed out and were drying off

when Rolf looked up. "Something's queer. Anyone notice the light?"

The sky seemed yellowish, and the air was very still. Funny little whorls of water spun on the cove's surface.

"I never saw it like that," Brother said.

"Probably only a haze." Parry was drying her hair.

"Right." Rolf threw down his towel. "I want to fill my water jugs. Let's go do it now — it'll take us all to carry them."

But Granpa was walking through the trees, and Brother jumped in and waded to meet him.

"I don't like the look of this at all," Granpa said without ceremony. "I believe a low pressure system is forming over the area."

Tim remembered words he'd heard on television weather reports. "You mean a storm is coming?"

"Not coming. Forming. Possibly right over our heads. I've been trying to get a report from town, but my radio is dead. I want you to pack up and get to the main island."

His voice had a tone of command they had never heard before, but to Mouse's surprise Rolf didn't object. "How much time do you think we have?" he said.

"I don't know. Maybe nothing will happen for half a day. Or this calm could shift at any minute and wind could start. So I want everyone out now, for safety's sake. And it would be a good idea for us to go together."

Rolf nodded. "I'm putting water aboard — I'll finish and meet you in the channel in half an hour."

Granpa beckoned "quick now" to Parry and Brother, who waded ashore. Rolf turned to pick up a jug as Granpa left, but Tim hesitated.

"You know," Tim said, "this could be some kind of trick. The weather looks weird, but he could be trying to get you to the mainland."

"I know." Rolf was lifting the big water bottles. "But I think he's right about the weather. I've never seen anything like this sky before. And whatever he's doing, this is a good way for me to leave." He straightened up and faced them. "I have to go. I really do."

Mouse's heart took a sudden dip. For all that she had said, now that the time had come she felt awful. All she could do was help carry the heavy jugs up to the spring and back and stow the water in the cabin. Tim helped Rolf tighten lines and tie things down, and Mouse checked below to make sure nothing was loose.

"I hope Captain Fisher's not having a fit looking for us," Tim said, breaking her silence as they waded ashore to get the skiff.

"He may not know about the sky." Mouse lifted the bushes off the skiff's stern.

"Of course he does, he lives with weather." Tim shoved the bow, which was stuck in the sand. It came loose with a loud sucking noise and the skiff shot out into the cove. They half ran, half waded after it and scrambled over the sides.

"Do you want a line?" Rolf called.

Tim shook his head. "But don't go too fast."

Rolf switched on the sloop's ignition and the *Windsong* moved out ahead of the skiff, the engines reverberating across the quiet cove. Together they entered the channel and chugged toward Granpa's side of the island. The water in the channel was dead calm, and even the sea beyond the reef scarcely moved. The sky seemed to be duller; its blue had turned to greyish tan, and the strange yellow light had dimmed. They could see Granpa's dinghy waiting for them.

"I'll head for the western side of the bay," Granpa called. "It's longer, but it's more protected if a wind hits. Stay close in case we run into problems."

He started up. Rolf brought the *Windsong* in behind him, and Tim moved as near to the sloop as he could without getting right in her wake. The three boats formed a line, hugging the reef. Mouse watched Granpa's hut fade out of sight and the islands fall behind. Then her eyes returned to Rolf ahead of them. What would it be like, to go alone to Mexico? How would he feel, what would he do? She tried to imagine his trip, his sitting alone in the cockpit, past island after island, across the huge, empty sea. But she couldn't.

She turned to Tim. "I wonder what Mexico's like," she said. "What do you think Rolf'll do there?"

"I'm more interested in what a forming storm is like," he said. "I don't know about Mexico."

He scanned the clouds, but still there was no wind. The water was so smooth it was almost oily looking, and he noticed a sea turtle floating on the surface behind *Windsong*'s stern.

Without warning, Rolf's sloop veered to port, and then they saw that Granpa, too, had made an almost right-angle turn into the bay.

Tim half rose. "What's he doing?" he shouted to Rolf. "I thought he said go all the way to the point."

"There's a whirlpool by the reef," he shouted. "A big one. Hurry. Turn."

Now Mouse could see a line of white where the water changed color, and Tim cut sideways, coming in alongside the *Windsong*.

"I think you should get aboard," Rolf said. "We can tow the skiff until we get nearer shore."

He caught Mouse's line and they scrambled into the cockpit. Clouds were hanging low over the western arm of the bay, and a long line of white water ran out to sea, with whitecaps foaming in front of it.

"That's a big tide," Tim said, scowling.

But Rolf was squinting at Granpa, who had begun to zigzag. "There's another whirlpool. I think they're all over the place — there must be crazy air currents above us."

The two boats were losing ground, although Granpa was still farther ahead. Dark clouds were all across the sky now, and to the west Mouse could see an ominous purple mass in the sky over the main island. Pearl-coloured plumes hung from the top of the thunderhead into the darker part below. Long streaks of lightning stood up and ran down the clouds, and hundreds of little specks, flocks of birds, were flying away from the main island rain forests. Mouse felt really frightened. She looked at Rolf. He had one knee on the bench, half standing, intently watching the water ahead.

"What can we do?" she said.

"Nothing. Keep going." He sounded tense.

Granpa had straightened out, and was chugging ahead into the bay. Everything was getting darker as the clouds came closer and settled lower over the surface of the water. They were boiling and churning, and Mouse began to feel a wind that rushed at them from first one side and then the other. It stopped and then it started again.

Tim turned to look at Granpa and Parry and Brother. Their white boat was a bright spot against the dark bay and sky. Near it, he saw a dark hump of water on the surface. It seemed to boil and bubble, and then, like a water fountain, it began to rise higher.

"What *is* that?" Mouse said. She heard a rushing noise, like a distant roaring.

"It's a waterspout." Rolf half rose. "Granpa's too close to it."

Granpa's dinghy turned sideways, trying to head backward. The *Windsong* turned too — Rolf was staying with him. The bubbling column stopped rising and hovered, then slowly lowered into the water. Rolf swung the *Windsong* hard, trying to reach Granpa. Suddenly, the column came up again. It made a peculiar moaning, hissing noise as Mouse and Tim and Rolf watched it rise higher and begin to move. It was heading for Granpa's dinghy. They saw Granpa pull Parry toward him and throw himself over Brother, and then he seemed to fly sideways as the dinghy spun up in the air and disappeared in a froth of foam.

"It's headed for us!" Rolf shouted. "Hang on!"

Mouse sat frozen. Her eyes travelled up the green column of water and her ears absorbed its unearthly rushing sound. The spout wavered up, down, and rose again to sway straight for their boat.

Desperately Rolf threw the *Windsong* into neutral and reversed the engine. He backed to one side, but it was almost as though the waterspout were alive and chasing them. They could feel its spray flying over their faces like fine rain, and see circular waves running out from its base. The *Windsong* began to buck, sucked straight for the waterspout's centre.

Mouse felt a sickening lurch, then a drop. The waterspout had shot to one side.

"It's falling on us!" Tim yelled.

Mouse closed her eyes. She bent over, waiting, and then she opened them again. The column suddenly seemed to drop in two, its upper half pulling up into clouds, the lower column dropping into the water. Then it dissipated into a thousand sheets of spray, leaving the *Windsong* rocking on a pond.

Rolf sat down.

"Wow," Tim said.

Mouse said nothing, afraid she was going to be sick.

Rolf gunned forward, looking for Granpa.

"There they are!" Tim pointed.

They could see the overturned dinghy, and then they spotted Granpa, clinging onto it and holding Brother with one arm.

"Brother's hurt!" he shouted. "Hurry!"

"Where's Parry? I don't see her!" Mouse ran to the bow and then she saw her, almost hidden in the water beside Granpa. Tim ran forward too and threw Granpa a line, and dropped the ladder.

Granpa lifted Brother up to them, and Parry followed as they laid Brother carefully on the deck. Brother's eyes were closed and blood oozed out of a gash on his head. Mouse ran to get a towel to wrap his head and noticed Rolf watching the sky.

"I feel more wind," he said. "Tell Tim to get forward and watch."

A fine mist flew everywhere. Parry began to shiver.

"How do you feel?" Mouse said.

"Okay," Parry said, "But I can't stop shaking."

They both looked at Brother. His eyes opened and he smiled weakly. Mouse thought he looked really small.

Suddenly they heard Tim shout. "Help's coming!"

Captain Fisher's biggest launch was speeding straight toward them across the water. Rolf turned, and for a split second his face tightened. Then he waved and pushed the throttle forward. In minutes the two boats reached each other and two men jumped aboard the sloop with a canvas sling. They put Brother in and carried him across, followed by Granpa and Parry. Captain Fisher leaned out to Rolf, his engines straining to cast loose.

"Follow me to the docks," he called. "Stay right with me."

Rolf nodded at him.

"Get on the launch," Rolf said to Tim and Mouse in an undertone.

"Good-bye," Mouse whispered as Tim swung up onto the launch's deck.

Rolf raised his fingers in a tiny salute that no one else saw. A pelting rain began to fall just as the last lines fell away. Rolf curved around in a tight circle, following the launch's wake.

For a minute Captain Fisher looked back and then, satisfied that Rolf was following closely, began to concentrate on steering. He peered through the mist and rain at the channel markers that led into the the town's docks, and he didn't notice the sloop falling slowly off, beginning to curve.

Then suddenly he did.

"That crazy kid!" he roared.

He hit the wheel with his fist, but he kept to his course.

"William, we'll get your grandson to the emergency clinic and then I'll get back here and get after him."

Mouse watched the *Windsong* finish her turn and leap ahead, careening around a buoy and flying across the bay. Rolf had cut the skiff loose, and it bobbed up and down in the channel behind them.

Captain Fisher gunned to the dock, yelling for Mr. Wade.

Now the *Windsong* was a distant blur through the mist and rain, so far out in the bay that they could barely see her hull.

Captain Fisher turned around. "Get in the car," he said to Tim and Mouse. "I'll talk to you later."

They climbed in, watching the men lift Brother, and made room for Parry. Then they turned again to the bay.

"I wonder if we'll ever see him again," Mouse said in a low voice.

But Captain Fisher heard her and turned around. "You can bet your boots on it," he said grimly. "I'm going to make jolly sure of that."

Twelve

Two hours later Captain Fisher strode into the hospital lobby, where Tim and Mouse were waiting in chairs.

"Now," he confronted them. "Where did that boy go? He must have said something. You were on his boat."

Tim stood up. "That's because he gave us a tow when we saw the whirlpools."

"He was just using the same islands we were, to camp out," Mouse added.

Captain Fisher frowned. "I've been monitoring the helicopter search patrol, but there's no sign of him. The pilots had to come back — too much turbulence. How's Brother?"

"He's okay," Tim said. "He had to have stitches, though. We were supposed to go in and see him when you got back."

"Let's go, then." Captain Fisher propelled them down the hall. "But keep in mind that you'll be doing that boy a favour if you figure out where he is."

Tim and Mouse looked at each other.

"We can't," Mouse said after a pause. "We really don't know."

"I suggest you try to remember," Captain Fisher said again as he knocked on the door of Brother's room.

Brother was sitting up in bed looking cheerful, with a big white bandage wrapped round his head. "I can leave tomorrow," he said.

"Glad to hear that." Captain Fisher smiled at him. "But you may not be able to." He turned to Granpa. "We've got a problem with the weather, William. Carib Storm Centre says it's going to be a big one. They can't tell which way it's going, either."

Granpa got up at once. "I'll come with you. I'd better put my people in motion."

They started into the hall, then Granpa looked back.

"All of you wait here. Don't bother the nurses, and help in any way you can. We'll see you later."

Their voices moved on down the hall, but not before the children clearly heard Captain Fisher say, "We've got boats after him, but I don't know how long they can stay out."

"I wouldn't worry about it too much, Jim," Granpa's voice replied. "The boy's a good sailor. He'll hole up somewhere."

Then they faded away, and Tim turned to Parry. "How could it be a hurricane? I thought they always come late in the summer."

"Not always," she said. "Sometimes they're early."

"Have you ever been in one?" Mouse scrambled onto the foot of Brother's bed.

Parry nodded. "It was scary. I'm scared now."

Tim had been feeling excited at the thought of a hurricane, but if Parry, who was usually fearless, was nervous, maybe it was worse than he had thought.

"I guess this building's safe . . ." he began.

"Of course it is," A nurse had bustled in to take Brother's temperature and feel his pulse. "And you're not to worry. Just take care of this fellow here."

She straightened Brother's sheets. "Best get off his bed, so as not to joggle him, that's good children. He should sleep a bit, if he wants to."

"I don't," Brother said. "I want to get up and see what's happening."

She laughed. "You can't. You have to rest."

She shooed Tim and Mouse and Parry into the waiting room, and Tim went to the window and hung out. The hospital did seem sturdy, two floors of thick stucco walls and a

red tile roof. Tim could hear hammering outside. People in the streets below were nailing
boards over windows and doors, and others
were closing their brightly painted shutters.
Now he understood those shutters — open,
they were pretty decorations against the pas-
tel buildings; closed, they fit snug and flat, seal-
ing the houses into tight, smooth boxes that
could ride out a storm. He turned to Parry.

"How strong can a hurricane wind get?"

"Strong. And sometimes there are tidal
waves."

"Oh."

Mouse closed her eyes, trying to picture Rolf
on the boat, the wind skittering all around.
She saw the sails, the sky, the sea. Then she
saw waves, swelling behind the stern, growing
into a huge wall of water, curving over the
boat. She shook her head.

"There's got to be something we can do,"
she said.

"There isn't." Parry walked over to a table
where there were books and games. "And we'd
better play something or they'll give us something to do we don't like."

By suppertime the town was closed up and
ready, and the head floor nurse, whose name
was Miss Owen, came to take Tim and Mouse
and Parry to the cafeteria.

212

"I can feel it coming," one of the nurses was saying as they sat down. "And it's going to be a bad one."

Miss Owen ignored her and got plates of ham and plantains and fried bananas, and saucers piled high with fruit.

"There's cake at the nurses' station," she told Parry. "We keep it there for midnight snacks, but you children are welcome to what we've got, as long as it lasts."

Tim looked at her. "Do you know if they found a boy, in a boat?" he asked.

"The one who brought you in." Miss Owen looked sympathetic. "We heard. No, but I'm sure they're doing all they can to find him."

"That's just the trouble," Mouse whispered to Parry as they walked back upstairs to Brother's room. "Part of me hopes they find him, and part of me doesn't."

Brother had fallen asleep after all, and they went back in the waiting room, feeling restless. The rain had stopped, and the sky looked green. Lightning flickered everywhere, and a kind of hush had fallen over the town. Miss Owen came in.

"Now we can use your help," she said. "Our shift is half strength, as some nurses can't get in tonight."

She took them down the hall and showed

them where things were kept, and then sent them in and out of patients' rooms taking water pitchers, picking up trays, telling what they knew about the storm. Mouse was surprised to find that she enjoyed it, and she was sorry when Miss Owen announced bedtime.

"Your grandfather has sent word that he wants you to stay here tonight too," the nurse said to Parry, "so we'll get out the cots."

She brought them extra pillows too, and they helped her swing the waiting room's heavy shutters shut. She flicked on a lamp and left. The room was strangely quiet.

I wonder what Rolf's doing, Mouse thought, and stopped. She somehow felt he had special knowledge, like seabirds and other wild things have, of what to do in awful storms. But she couldn't picture where he was and she didn't want to say anything silly. Instead she jumped on her cot.

"This hospital's better than the ones at home." She stretched out and wiggled her shoes off.

"What ones at home?" Tim peeled off his shirt. "How many have you been to?"

"Well, not that many. But I bet they'd never let us all sleep in the same room."

"They would if they had a hurricane," he said. "They don't have hurricanes."

"But they have blizzards. People get stranded in airports." She knew that wasn't good enough. "And . . ."

Parry stopped the argument. "I'd like to see a blizzard."

"They're great." Tim sat down. "The snow goes sideways, and it gets deeper and deeper, sometimes ten feet."

Parry tried to picture it, but she couldn't. Mouse tried to help.

"It's all cold and howling and grey and white. It's sort of fun, but it's still not as nice as here. I'd like to live here. We could go to school." She had visions of a big room with open windows, breezes, swimming at recess.

Parry smiled. "We'd be in the same class."

"Do you think there's any chance we *could* live here?" Mouse turned to Tim. "Because of Dad's business?"

"I don't know, probably not." Tim went to the window to look out.

"What do you do here at Christmas?" Mouse was still planning.

"Regular things," Parry said. "Presents, church — what do you do?"

"Same."

They pulled their cots together. For an hour they told each other everything they could think of about the way they lived, how it was alike, how it was different. Then they began on their families, and finally what they wanted to do when they were bigger.

Mouse was getting dreamy. "I might like to be a nurse." She was thinking of what Miss Owen did.

"I'd rather be a doctor," Parry said. She yawned. "Maybe a doctor for fish, so I could be a diver too."

"When I was six I ate a butterfly," Tim said suddenly.

"That sounds gross. Why?"

"I don't know, I wanted to see what it tasted like."

"What did it?"

"Sticks. I threw up."

Now they were really sleepy, and they began to talk about Rolf.

"If only we knew where he was," Tim said.

"I wish we were on his boat." Mouse felt suddenly close to tears. "I wonder if he liked us."

Tim looked surprised. "Why wouldn't he?"

"I don't know." Mouse stopped, not sure why she had said it. "He never said much."

"That's because he didn't have a family,"
Parry said firmly. "I think he did like us. I
think he's missing us now."

Rolf had counted on not being followed for
a little while. But even so, he had breathed a
sigh of relief as he shot through the reef and
onto the open ocean, heading west. The haze
had deepened, and the purple clouds had settled lower, so that soon he was hidden from
land by the mist and pouring rain. There was
still no wind, but the sloop's engine was running well, and he pushed her as fast as he
could. He couldn't remember ever seeing such
queer weather, but then he had never seen
the start of a hurricane either, if that's what
this was. At least he knew that hurricanes
usually moved north — maybe he could get
away from this one by going south.

The whitecaps beyond the point had sub-
sided and there were no whirlpools out here
in the open ocean, but still his eyes ranged all
around, in front, port and starboard, astern.
He was soaking wet but he stayed standing
in the cockpit until he was certain there
weren't any more strange-looking currents.
Then he sat down again, the rain running
down his face and his clothes plastered to his

body. Zec rode at the top of the companion-way, walking back and forth. Rolf had never seen the gull so nervous. He hoped it wasn't a bad sign.

"Don't worry, Zec." He made his voice sooth-ing. "This weather is a good thing — it'll keep Captain Fisher busy. We're going to make it to Mexico. Nothing can stop us now."

He knew he was taking a chance being so far from land, even though he was parallel-ing it. But if the wind picked up they could al-ways head straight in. Also, if anyone did start looking for him, they would surely ex-pect him to be closer to shore, or hiding along the coastline's endless bays or coves or beaches.

By late afternoon he was far to the south, halfway to the southern tip of the main is-land. The rain was heavy as ever, and Zec was still restless — maybe some food would help calm him. Rolf got dried fish from a bucket, and then he realized how long it had been since he himself had eaten — not since breakfast. He remembered Tim's fish. How long ago that seemed! He could hardly believe it had been only that morning, in bright calm sunshine, with everybody laughing and fooling around. He remembered Mouse's happy shrieks when he threw her overboard, and Tim hauling the jugs, wishing him luck. Parry diving with him, and Brother like a cheerful, bouncing ball. And Granpa, his strong voice calm and firm, saying things that Rolf liked.

Rolf felt a strange empty pain, an ache he didn't understand. He sank back on the cockpit bench, huddled against the rain, wondering what was wrong. He thought of his mother, and shook his head. Then he thought of his house, his room, his mother again, and finally, his father.

"I can't stand it without him, Zec," he said suddenly. "I just can't."

His voice choked, and he found himself fighting blinding tears. Then he stopped fighting and began to sob, coughing, flooding sobs that went on and on, heard only by the sea and the solemn sea gull, his tears mingling down his face with the rain.

After a long time, he stopped. Even later, he raised his head and looked around. He could see a current beginning to move, and the weather was definitely getting worse. The dark clouds had a strange greenish hue, and ahead lay the open Caribbean in all its empty vastness. It would be better to find an anchorage for the night, and wait until morning to tackle it.

He shook himself, drops of water flying in all directions, and reached across to a locker for a towel. He dried off and headed the *Windsong* closer to shore. He cruised along the shore for another thirty minutes before he found what he was looking for — a tiny bay, where palm trees hung out over the water and white sand gleamed among their trunks. He brought the sloop in and anchored, and set the tiller. Listlessly he began to secure her, going over her lines and hull again so that she could ride out a storm.

Then he sighed. He knew he ought to be feeling marvelous. He had stocked up and he had repaired his boat. He had gotten away from Captain Fisher, and he was on his way to Mexico. But his heart felt heavy, and even his legs and arms felt like lead. He looked around. This was a beautiful lagoon. Even in this weather, if the others were here they would go swimming. Then they would eat, and play some crazy game, probably.

"But they're not," he said aloud, startled at how dull his voice sounded. He went below and made a sandwich and brought it up to the cockpit. But suddenly he could feel his tears starting again, and he threw the sandwich overboard. He walked up and down the deck, pacing until he could breathe again.

Then he went below. He lit the lamp, unrolled his charts, bent over them, and with a sigh sat down and began to read.

At midnight, finally, slowly, the wind began to rise. At first it merely gusted, flipping sudden bursts along the streets and around the roofs of the town. But hour after hour it grew stronger, flattening bushes and trees as it spread its power across the hills. It roared out across the sea, turning the flat surface into a large racing chop that by dawn had churned to a fury of pounding waves.

Mouse and Tim woke up to hear a moaning, whining howl. Mouse squinted through the shutters and caught her breath. The trees outside the window were bent flat to the ground and the rain was blowing straight sideways out of dark, boiling clouds. While she watched, a roof went off a house across the street like a matchbox cover. Stunned, she came back to the cots and woke Tim.

"There's no way Rolf's going to be all right," Tim said when he looked out.

"We've got to tell," Mouse said.

"She's right," Parry said, as they went in Brother's room. "Let's find Miss Owen."

But the nurse was nowhere around, and only one person was at the main nursing station. She looked up.

"Oh, good," she said. "I'm needing you — we're very short-handed. We have trays to collect, and after that Miss Owen wants you to go to the children's ward and organize them into games. And we'll need you for messages too — we've switched to the generator and we don't want to overload it with intercoms. Come on."

But Mouse caught her arm.

"Is there some way to find Captain Fisher?" she said. "We have to talk to him."

The nurse shook her head. "I'm sorry, dear. The phone lines are out. You'll have to wait till he comes over here. Oh, and your brother," she said to Parry as she looked at her charts, "can get up. Will you be a dear and walk around with him for a bit — make sure he's not going to get dizzy."

Parry nodded.

"You two come with me." She bustled Mouse and Tim down the hall. "No one's contagious," she added as she walked into a large room, where at least a dozen boys and girls of all ages were in beds around the walls.

Mouse felt shy. "What do you want us to do?"

"Just watch out for them — try to keep them quiet, and don't act frightened about the hurricane."

"Games," Tim muttered, and walked over to three of the oldest boys. "Any of you guys play Monopoly?"

Mouse decided to read aloud to some younger children. They seemed glad to see her, and she sat down and started a story about a wild horse in Australia. It was good, and for a time she was absorbed in the ranch and the family she was reading about.

But all the time the wind outside was getting stronger, tearing at the docks and the town like a hungry animal, and Mouse began to glance through a narrow crack in the shutters. Soon she was unable to stop wondering what was happening outside.

"Come on!" some little kid said. "That's the fifth time you've forgotten your place!"

Mouse looked at him. "You read." She handed the book to the oldest one. "I'll be back in a minute."

She ran down the hall to Brother's room. Brother was up, wearing shorts. "We've got to do *something*," Mouse said to Parry.

"They might have a radio," Brother said.

Mouse stared at him. "A radio. Why didn't we think of that?"

"I should have," Parry said. "Come on. Let's find Miss Owen."

It took them twenty minutes to locate her, in the operating room where there was an emergency, and another half hour of waiting before she came out. When Parry explained, Miss Owen nodded. "Come with me."

She led them to the basement along a corridor filled with pipes and boilers, and into a room. There stood a noisy, humming marine radio.

Miss Owen fiddled with the knobs until one voice rose above the squeals and hums.

"Here." She handed Mouse the mike. "He's on. Go ahead."

"Captain Fisher?" Mouse shouted.

"Yes, what is it?" Captain Fisher's voice crackled from the box.

Mouse cleared her throat. "We remembered that boy said something about going south. We thought maybe you'd want to know."

"South?" They could hear the strain even above the static. "That's been the worst part of the storm." There was a pause. "We'll alert our people" — Captain Fisher came back on — "but I'm afraid there's not much we can do until the wind drops. Are you all right?"

"Yes, we're fine," Mouse said. "But isn't there any way a boat could go out? A big boat?"

"No." He almost barked the word. "The wind is a hundred miles an hour."

"A hundred miles an hour?" Parry said as Mouse slowly put the mike down.

They stared at each other, and Mouse's eyes filled with tears. "We shouldn't have done it," she said. "We shouldn't have done any of it. Now there's no way to rescue him at all."

Thirteen

The wind woke Rolf up. A big gust hit the sloop and sent her heeling, and then another spun her hard on the anchor line. She came up short with a violent jerk, and Rolf jumped off his bunk. In one quick motion he fumbled for the electric lantern, flicked on the beam and leaped on deck, shocked as the wind's blast hit him. Instinctively he ducked back into the cockpit. Then he raised his head and trained the lantern's beam on shore.

He was much farther out than he had been last night. His moorings weren't holding, he thought. Then he realized it was the water that had moved higher — the beach was flooded and the water was racing up among the palm tree trunks.

I should have got a better mooring last night, he thought. One that was okay for a wind like this. Then he shook his head. Thinking like that wouldn't help matters. He had never seen a sea like this, and he probably wouldn't have known how to prepare for it. The important thing was to figure out what to do now, not worry about what he should have done last night.

His eyes roamed idly over Zec, huddled on the bench, only half awake. If the sea was racing in, Rolf's best bet was to move the sloop in too, in among the trees if need be. He could probably brace her, find some place where she wouldn't take too much pounding. But how?

He thought a minute more. He couldn't raise the anchor. He needed it as a brake, or the sloop would hurl herself in to shore and wreck. He had to get her in slowly, and that meant dragging the anchor, if he could.

He checked his watch. It was three o'clock — an hour and a half till daylight. It would be safer to wait, but he couldn't. The wind was rising, and thudding waves were hitting the boat harder every minute.

"I'll be really careful, Zec," he said. Hearing his voice aloud gave him courage, and he hung the lantern on the wall and got a flashlight. Then he tied a long line around his waist and went out into the cockpit again. He tied the other end of his belt line to a cleat and dropped the coils in the cockpit so it would pay out without fouling. Now there was nothing to do but go.

He dropped on his hands and knees and moved slowly onto the deck. He felt a stab of fear — the flashlight's beam seemed tiny in the blackness, and the gusts of wind and the rushing water were terrifying.

He talked to himself. "I've got to do it," he said. "I can't be scared." But it seemed an endless journey to the bow. At last he reached the anchor line. It was tight as a drum. Rolf tugged at it, and his heart sank. The anchor was doing just what it should be doing — holding fast. It was in so tight that it was probably caught on a rock. In calm water that wouldn't have been a problem; he could have dived in and pulled it free. But in this wind and current, the *Windsong*'s whole weight was on the line. There was no way he could pull it loose.

He lay flat, trying to decide what to do. If he got his spare anchor, he could put its line on the winch, hang it overboard, and cut the main anchor loose. Then he could let the second anchor line out slowly, so it would just drag the bottom, and with luck he could maneuver the sloop inshore.

It took a long time to get back with the

knife and the second anchor. In the dark the wind seemed like something alive, growing stronger all the time, its gusts like a giant's breath that seemed to create a vacuum and suck his own air away.

I can't think like that, he told himself. I've got to keep moving. Finally he reached the forward winch again. He got the new line on it and dropped the new anchor overboard. He let it down carefully so it wouldn't catch deep on the bottom. Then he locked the winch handle, and edged out onto the bow and pulled his knife from its scabbard. He began to saw at the main anchor's big nylon line, and the knife seemed to make no impression at all. The wind hit a blast on his back that almost flipped him over. He gasped, and his free hand grabbed his lifeline. Then he went back to sawing with the knife. It was too slow. The strong nylon line was made to hold, and he seemed to be barely denting it. Once more he made the long arduous journey back along the deck, crawling desperately now, to the cockpit and the cabin. He had two pairs of wire cutters in his cabin toolbox and he stuck the larger pair in his shorts. For a minute he hesitated. Who would know if he went overboard? Who would help him? There's no one but Zec, he thought, and he can't do anything. Then he thought of his father, and how calm he would have been in an emergency like this. And how well he would have handled it. I'll do the same, Rolf said grimly to himself.

He started back to the bow again, the flashlight in one hand, the outside hand gripping the deck rail against the wind. He reached the bow at last and reached for the main anchor line. He got the clippers around it. He squeezed. The line parted. The anchor fell away and the boat gave a lurch as it shot with the water toward the beach. Then it lurched just as hard as it slowed, held by the spare anchor.

"So far so good," Rolf muttered.

He eased his body slightly back against the shelter of the cabin front, and unlocked the winch handle. He turned it slowly, letting out line. The coil on the deck threatened to blow overboard at any minute, so Rolf pulled it over and sat almost on top of it.

It was hard to see, because the sloop was moving inshore stern first, and he had to stop, take one hand off the winch, shine the torch backward past the stern, and watch the trees on shore come closer. By now the water was so high that the only way he could tell where the beach had been was by the branches of the tree trunks, rising out of the water.

Lucky this anchor line is so long, he thought, and lucky it's dragging — and it could still hit an underwater snag and catch, like the first one. But so far it was moving, and they were getting closer to the trees.

About twenty feet from the trees, he stopped paying out line. He locked the winch again and flattened himself back into the cockpit. He picked up a line he had left there, and struggled onto the stern. The boat moved slowly backward, the dragging anchor still keeping her under control. He would have to be quick. He dropped the fender pads over the side. The stern hit a tree with a hard bump. Rolf fended off — he wanted the sloop farther into the trees. Now they were bumping into other trunks, but still Rolf waited, until, when he shone the torch ahead, he could see land among the trunks. He was ten feet away from a big palm, seven feet, five, and then quick as a flash he grabbed the trunk and slid the line around it, making a loop fast. He ran forward and grabbed a branch of another tree, stopping the sloop just long enough for him to loop the bow line around the second trunk. The *Windsong* kept moving for only a minute, and then the line tightened, groaned, and held.

Rolf crouched, panting, soaking wet. If the trees stay up, he thought, we'll be all right. If the wind doesn't tear the sloop to pieces, if I can stay awake. Those are big ifs. The boat was vibrating all over, and while he was moving her, the wind had changed from gusts to a steady roar. It *is* a hurricane, Rolf thought. And a bad one at that.

He crawled into the cabin. He lit the lantern again and sat, still heaving, on the bunk. When he had caught his breath he got up and changed his clothes and made himself eat something while he waited for daylight. His eyes focused on Zec, now balancing on the companionway. The gull looked wet and miserable.

"Don't worry, Zec. She's holding."

When the cabin began to lighten into dim greyness, Rolf hauled himself wearily to his feet again, and reached for his slicker. He knew he had to put out double mooring lines, and he had better do it now. Just before he went out he spoke to Zec again.

"Dad always said she could ride out a hurricane. Now she'll really be put to the test."

* * *

"Get up," Mouse heard Tim say. She opened her eyes. A whole day and another night had passed again. Tim was at the window. "It's stopping."

Mouse and Parry slid off their cots and ran to throw open the shutters. A sodden landscape lay below, covered with puddles, downed trees, branches, and debris. But Tim was right, the wind had slowed to a stiff breeze, and the clouds were high, scudding off across the bay.

"Now they can start looking for him," Mouse said.

"They're probably out already," Parry said.

Tim and Mouse walked after her into Brother's room where Miss Owen was already at work, checking Brother's stitches.

"They're fine," she said. "You only need an adhesive patch today."

Deftly she put on the smaller bandage and then she gave Brother a cheery pat. "You'll probably be leaving today too, after the doctor sees you."

She turned around. "Now. The rest of you are not to worry about your friend. If he was smart enough to get through a waterspout, I'm sure he's come through the hurricane too. I'm sure Captain Fisher will have word of him."

But when Captain Fisher arrived at the hospital his face was grim.

"There's no sign of the boy, nor of the boat either," he said. "The Coast Patrol's been looking since dawn. But I did get a radio message to your parents that you're all right. They'll call as soon as the telephones work, probably this afternoon."

He ushered Tim and Mouse to his car and nosed it out of the hospital's entryway. This morning he couldn't drive at his usual breakneck speed; the streets were close to impassable, and frequently he had to back up and turn around and find another route.

People were all over the streets, too, cleaning up the mess and opening their houses. As the car twisted and turned. Mouse began to get one of her funny feelings. She could somehow see Rolf doing the same thing — cleaning off his decks, bailing water from the cockpit, raising his sails. But then she stopped short. If he was all right he would be leaving, and she would never see him again. Her feelings were all tangled up together and she shook her head in the usual gesture she used to clear her head.

"I don't know what we'll find at the house," Captain Fisher was saying. "I hope Mrs. Shaw's all right."

The first thing they found was that the driveway had disappeared. Four big palm trees were down on it, their branches covering the road. They had to leave the car and walk.

"Well, at least the house is still standing," Captain Fisher said as they came out in front. "Very fortunate. Very fortunate."

A quick tour around the outside showed he was right — four trees down, a garden hedge smashed, the toolshed demolished, and another big tree down beside the verandah. But there was no major damage, and soon Mrs. Shaw and two men from the Salvage Company arrived.

"Nothing's too bad inside either," Captain Fisher told them.

A tree had smashed against the shutters and broken the windows behind, but every single branch had missed the roof.

"We'll just go to work then, and be cleaned up in no time," Mrs. Shaw said.

The men went to work outside, pulling branches aside, hauling trees away, propping shrubs back up, and Tim and Mouse helped Mrs. Shaw on the inside, accomplishing a lot with rags and towels. By noon Captain Fisher felt satisfied.

"That's about all we can do now," he said. "We'll wait for things to dry when the sun comes out."

He decided to go in town and check with the Coast Patrol again, and as soon as he left, Tim and Mouse hopped on their bikes.

They pedalled as fast as they could, out of the driveway and down to the coast road. Parry had told them Granpa's house was past the hotel. It seemed funny to be heading toward the hotel. It hadn't really been that long ago, Mouse reflected as she pedalled, but it seemed as though it had been a year since they had been driving on that same road with Mom and Dad, wondering who the white-haired boy was, and noticing his boat.

"How much farther is it?" Mouse was out of breath.

"I don't know. Parry said the driveway was above the next beach."

When they came around a curve a house was spread out before them. It was large and Spanish style. It looked familiar.

"It's the same house!" Mouse breathed. "The one with the garden and the dog that I went to the day Rolf jumped you at the cliff."

Tim stared. "You mean they *live* there?"

Parry and Brother were waiting at the big front door.

"I can't believe this is your house." Mouse leaned her bike up against the wall.

"Why not?" Parry said.

"It's just that we were here before, before we knew you," Tim said, struggling with his kick stand. "You've got a big dog," he added.

"It's a watchdog," Brother said.

"How's your head?" They all felt shy.

"It's fine." He grinned the old Brother grin. "It doesn't hurt."

There was a silence. "They still can't find him," Parry said. "I overheard Granpa on the phone. He thinks the boat may have sunk."

"Oh."

They automatically looked at the sky, and the sea. There was much less breeze now, and the clouds seemed to be lighter. But still the sky was eerie-looking, and they couldn't bear to think of the *Windsong* under water, or smashed to pieces, and Rolf lying somewhere, or worse, floating . . .

"Is Granpa here?" Mouse asked.

"No, he'll be back in an hour or so," Brother said.

"Let's go down to the beach then," Tim said.

They started down the same path that Tim and Mouse had run up so long ago, looking for a white-haired boy who had jumped them for his sea gull. Then they hadn't even met Rolf, been on a boat, or known anything. Now they knew a lot about boats, they had seen a hurricane, and Rolf was gone. Mouse saw Tim run his fingers through his hair, almost exactly the way Rolf did it, but she said nothing. They had been talking about Rolf enough. Better to do something, anything they could think of.

They walked into the palm trees at the base of the cliff, and suddenly Parry stopped, pointing at the ground.

"A bird," Tim said. It was hard to see in the dim light.

"It's dead," Parry said.

"Oh."

Tim bent down. He had never seen one like it before. It was brown, with a short beak, shaped like a sea gull. It was lying on its side with one wing stretched out, looking peacefully asleep. "What kind is it?"

"It's a sora." Brother had stooped over. "They migrate from South America, I think. They go to Canada or somewhere."

Tim picked it up, and it rolled loosely in his

hand, its neck flapping. Mouse hung back, not wanting to look, and Parry took it and put it down again, gently folding the wing until it looked as though it was only waiting to wake up and fly away. They left it there, in the pink light under the trees.

"Do you ever think about dying?" Tim said to Parry as he walked.

"Yes, but it scares me," Parry said.

"Oh, I don't mean the dying part, but what happens when you have to live forever," Tim said. "What do you suppose there is to do?"

"I don't know." She smiled. "I hope you can swim."

They had reached the base of the cliff and without speaking they began to climb, helping each other up the hard parts until they reached the ledge just under the top. There was the bay spread out before them, with hurricane wreckage along every beach. There was the hotel, the town, and, miraculously, their mangrove islands, still green beside the reef.

"The reef's what saved them," Parry said. "They look flooded, though."

Suddenly Mouse wanted to see the cove. She started across the top of the cliff, and this time she didn't look down at the tops of the palm trees, so she didn't have to close her eyes. She reached the far side, the others behind her, and then she looked down at the water, remembering the first time they had seen the *Windsong*. Mouse was imagining the sloop was there now, and then she blinked.

A sailboat was in the cove, anchored where Rolf had always kept the *Windsong*.

"It's him!" Tim almost screamed it. "It's Rolf!"

They stood rooted for only an instant before they began to run, sliding and leaping down the path, their bodies going so fast they almost fell. They were shouting as they ran, and a figure on the boat looked up and gave an answering shout. He dove into the water, and everyone reached the beach together.

"You're okay," Tim said.

"Yes." Rolf pushed his dripping hair back and turned and looked at the sloop. "I don't know how she came through it. But she did."

"What happened?"

"I decided not to go."

"Good," Tim said, and Mouse smiled.

"But what happened in the storm?" Brother demanded.

They walked into the water and stood, letting their arms float, while Rolf told them how he had had to sleep in snatches, and pick the right time to start up and go out with the receding waves. While he talked they could hear tiny swishes as the tide slid over the beach, and the sun came out at last and covered them in floods of golden light.

"That was after it got to be daylight," Rolf finished. "And then I had to wait until it got calm enough to get through the reef, before I came back here."

"That's really good," Mouse said. "Now all we need a new place to hide you, and . . ."

"That won't be necessary," a voice said.

They whirled. Granpa was standing on the path, and instinctively Parry ran forward, as if to protect Rolf.

"Granpa, no . . ."

But Granpa was not looking angry. "He can stay with me," he went on, "as long as he likes."

They stared at him, their mouths open.

"But what about Captain Fisher?" Tim said finally. "And the All Points Bulletin?"

"I think we can work that out." Granpa turned to Rolf. "Especially if I invite you officially. After all, very few grown men would head into a waterspout to rescue people the way you did. You have a lot of courage."

"Not enough," Rolf said. Suddenly his face

seemed to crumple. "Not enough to go south, and do what my father planned. And be alone."

Granpa was unperturbed. He stepped in front of Rolf, blocking him from view. "You have a lot of courage," he repeated. "Your mother thinks so too. In fact, she wants to tell you herself."

Rolf walked away along the beach, his voice tight. "She didn't love him. She never even cried. All she ever said was be brave, be brave."

Granpa walked after him, and put a gentle hand on his back. "Maybe she's saying that to herself," he said. "Have you ever thought of that? Maybe she needs you, more than you think."

Rolf shook his head, and walked a few steps farther. They all stood waiting, the breeze blowing their hair and making the palm trees sway. Rolf turned around.

"I guess I'll call her," he said.

"Good." Granpa started for the path. "We'll all go up. You must be hungry, too."

A phone was ringing when they walked in the house.

"That will be your father," Granpa said to Tim and Mouse. "Take it in the library."

"Tim?" Dad's voice was brisk, and Tim took a deep breath.

"Yes. Hi, Dad, how are you?"

"Fine. We're relieved you're all right. I've talked to Captain Fisher. He tells us you've met the Prime Minister."

"The who?" Static was heavy on the phone, and even with shouts it was hard to hear.

"The Prime Minister, Mr. Umlatta. The man you rescued from the waterspout," Dad went on briskly, while Tim tried to take in what he was saying. "In fact, Captain Fisher says Mr. Umlatta's quite fond of you. That seems to be one of the reasons he wants to talk to us about the bauxite."

"Mr. Umlatta? You mean Granpa? *He's* the Prime Minister?" Tim's voice rose in astonishment, steadily up the scale.

"Yes. Didn't you know?"

"No," Tim shouted. "He never said anything."

"He wouldn't," Dad answered. "He's that kind of person. One of the finest statesmen in the Western Hemisphere, but very modest. Captain Fisher says they're expecting him to win the election easily, too. Give him my best."

"We will," Tim shouted. "And Dad, we can't wait to see you. We've got a lot to tell you."

"I bet you have." Tim could hear his father's warm laugh across the miles, and he realized how much he missed him, and Mom too.

"Mom and I can't wait to see you either," Dad said.

Tim put down the phone, shaking his head. "Granpa's the Prime Minister," he said, turning to Mouse.

"I was standing here while you hogged the phone. I heard you."

Now the room itself was beginning to come into focus. Everywhere there were the trappings of government — framed certificates, three telephones, mementos, big pads, photographs lining the walls and on the desk in silver frames.

"Look," Tim said. "Here's one of him and the President."

"Uhff," Mouse let out her breath slowly, and sat down. "What'll we do?"

"I don't know. Just try to act normal, I guess." Tim left the desk. "Anyway, Mom and Dad are catching a plane in an hour, and they'll be here by midnight."

After supper — Granpa had invited them all — Tim and Mouse pedalled along the coast road again, but this time it was different. This time the breeze had gone altogether, and the light turned its sunset colours on their faces.

The air was warm and soft, and they looked at the sea, some colour now of clear dark they could not separate from the eastern sky. Stars were coming out.

"I think I want to stay here always," Mouse said.

"I'd like to stay here too," Tim said. "But we'd grow up. Suppose we grew up and wanted to leave?"

"We'd never feel that way."

"Parry wants to leave, she told me."

"But Rolf doesn't."

Mouse wondered what Rolf was doing. Probably sunset sailing, she thought. Anyone would be, anyone who knew what it was like tonight, anyone like Rolf. Sailing on and on across the reef and out into the violet sea. And suddenly she wanted to be out there too, not knowing where they were going and not caring, only knowing that wherever they went would be even more exciting than the places before, that something marvellous would always happen. That they would become tribe leaders, and find their food, that they would dive beneath the sea or go swimming, hearing nothing, seeing nothing except for the breeze and the whispers of the water that cradled them, and the call of the seabirds above their heads. They could live like birds, or become priests or Aztecs, or anything in the world.

Her bike hit a rock and she fell off.

Tim came back. "What's the matter with you? You weren't looking."

"I was." She hauled herself up, embarrassed. "Just not at the road, that's all."

After that she paid more attention, but she was still feeling restless when they reached Captain Fisher's house, and she hardly heard Mrs. Shaw say that Captain Fisher would be late.

They fooled around a while but it was hard to settle down, so they went upstairs. All of a sudden they got very sleepy. They tried to stay awake to wait up for Mom and Dad, but they couldn't. The next thing they knew Mom and Dad were in their room, shaking them gently, hugging them, listening to everything, making plans. When Mom finally called a halt to the talking, she smiled.

"Hey, everything's back to normal," she said. "Dad and I are here now. We can finish this conversation at breakfast."

She was right. When Tim's alarm went off he ran downstairs, and there were Mom and

Dad discussing the office as usual, and eating their usual eggs.

"Eat yours too, Mouse," Mom said automatically.

"Right," Tim whispered. "You need your protein. This morning you're going sailing with a white-haired pygmy."

Mouse giggled. "And something exciting might happen," she said.

Tim laughed, and stood up. Outside the door the blue sky beckoned, and the sailing breeze was perfect.

"Something already has," he said.